"To my beloved granddaughter, Miss Mary Claire St. James DeWinter, my sole surviving grandchild"—as if poor, disowned Phillip no longer existed—"the house at Westfield Court and all my remaining possessions and assets—" Edna St. James sat very straight in her chair and glared balefully at her niece, and several of the others gasped, but Mr. Prentice was not finished. "Providing only that she fulfill two necessary stipulations. Firstly, that she permit my daughter-in-law, Mrs. Edna Carrington St. James, widow of my beloved son Marcus, to remain in residence at Westfield Court for as long as she lives, and secondly, that she, as a young woman in need of protection and guidance, marry within one year of my death and remain married. If she fails to marry within the stipulated time or is divorced or widowed and fails to remarry within a year, Westfield Court and the entire estate is bequeathed to the State of Massachusetts for whatever purposes it may deem fit."

Everyone stared at Mary Claire. She was so white her scars were more visible in contrast, and Neil half rose from his chair in case she was about to faint.

Bridges

by

Linda Griffin

Bridges

Cover Art by *Jennifer Greeff*

The Wild Rose Press, Inc.
PO Box 708
Adams Basin, NY 14410-0708
Visit us at www.thewildrosepress.com

Publishing History
First Edition, 2022
Trade Paperback ISBN 978-1-5092-4181-1
Digital ISBN 978-1-5092-4182-8

Published in the United States of America

Dedication

To my wonderful editor, "Doctor" Nan Swanson,
who has expertly delivered my fictional children
and never flinched at the challenges.

Acknowledgments

I would like to thank Jennifer Greeff for her wonderful cover art, everyone at the Wild Rose Press, and Will Lamartine Thompson (1847-1909) for his beautiful hymn.

Chapter One

March 1963

The old man was dying, and everyone knew it, so things were topsy-turvy at Westfield Court.

When Neil Vincent was summoned to Mrs. St. James's large, cheerless study, she was nervously pacing before the desk as she gave orders to Mr. Lennox, the butler. She was a tall, sallow woman with neatly coiffed white hair, always impeccably dressed. Neil didn't like her, but she wasn't difficult to work for.

"Oh, Vincent," she said when she realized he was standing in the doorway. "Miss DeWinter is arriving earlier than expected. She'll be on the 8:58 train. Can you make that?"

He glanced at his watch. "Yes, ma'am."

"Very good," she said and turned back to Mr. Lennox.

Neil wanted to ask how he would recognize Miss DeWinter, but Mrs. St. James had already forgotten his existence. He didn't think of himself as a servant but didn't mind that she did. With his military background, the stilted forms of address she expected came naturally enough.

"I don't suppose she'll be bringing a maid," she said to Mr. Lennox. "Jane will have to look after her."

Neil smiled to himself as he went out. Jane

wouldn't like the extra work, but she would enjoy handling the visitor's clothes. She loved fashion. She loved him, too, in her way, although he hadn't encouraged her. He liked to take things as they came.

On the drive to Brierly Station, he didn't speculate about who Miss DeWinter might be. It wasn't his job to know who she was, only to meet her train and take her safely back to Westfield Court. She wouldn't be the last of the friends and relatives who would gather as the old man's life came to its long-awaited and peaceful end.

Brierly was bustling today, as restless as the St. James household. He was in plenty of time for the train and sat in the car reading. The car was a Bentley Mark VI, as well-maintained and highly polished as it was the day it was purchased. The book he was reading was Thomas Hardy's *The Return of the Native*.

When the train rumbled in, he got out of the car. He stood patiently on the platform as the passengers disembarked, holding up a small slate on which he had chalked DEWINTER in large capitals. There weren't many passengers, but they were briefly delayed while the conductor helped a blind woman navigate the steps. Neil's gaze fell expectantly on a woman in her thirties, with an awful hat, but she was immediately met by a portly man and a teenage boy. No other likely prospects appeared, and he waited for someone to respond to the sign. No one did.

Finally, only two passengers were left on the platform—a small, homely man and the blind woman. Blind girl, really. She couldn't be more than twenty. She had a jointed white cane, and her large sunglasses didn't cover the edges of the scars on her face. She would not have been beautiful even without the scars—

too thin, for starters, of average height but with small bones. On the other hand, her face might once have been pretty, and her hair was clean and shining, raven black, and well brushed. She was too pale, and the scars around her eyes were red and ugly. She looked a little lost.

Feeling foolish, he lowered the slate. "Miss DeWinter?" he asked as he approached her.

"Yes," she said, turning toward his voice with a smile.

"I'm Vincent," he said. "The St. James chauffeur."

"Pleased to meet you, Mr. Vincent," she said. "Thank you for coming for me." Her voice was soft, her enunciation perfect.

The porter fetched her luggage—a single gray vinyl suitcase with a flower decal—from the depot and turned it over to Neil with a cheerful nod. Jane would be disappointed, especially if the girl's other clothes were as plain as what she wore, a simple dark dress with long sleeves and an unfashionable, below-the-knees hemline. "Would you take my arm?" he asked, positioning himself so she could place her hand in the crook of his elbow, which she did with easy confidence.

"Do you have a Christian name?" she asked.

"Yes, miss. It's Neil."

"That's a good name," she said. "Mine is Mary Claire. How is my grandfather, do you know?"

Neil, who hadn't known the old man had any grandchildren, said, "Hanging on, miss."

He opened the rear passenger door and helped her into the back seat.

"You don't have to call me 'miss' all the time," she said. "Please call me Mary Claire. Or my friends at school call me Sunny."

"Yes, miss," he said automatically and closed the door. He put her suitcase in the trunk. It wasn't very heavy. In the front seat, he adjusted the mirrors and started the car. "Would you like me to stop anywhere else?" he asked.

"No, thank you," she said. "Straight back to Westfield Court. Have you worked there very long?"

"Three years, miss."

She made a small sound of amusement but said nothing. He glanced at her in the rearview mirror, and she was leaning back, relaxed and smiling a little. Yes, she might have been pretty if not for those angry red scars. As they drove along the river, the route so familiar he could do it in his sleep, he glanced at her more than once. Finally, she said, "It's all right to ask, Mr. Vincent."

"I beg your pardon, miss?"

"I can feel you looking at me. It's all right to ask about the scars. I'm used to it."

"I wasn't looking at you," he lied. "It's not my place to ask questions, miss."

"Your place?" She was amused. "Do you like this job?"

"Yes, miss." Was she threatening him?

"Why?"

"Why, miss?" He glanced at her again.

"Oh, please," she said. "I've asked you to call me Mary Claire. May I call you Neil?"

"If you like…Mary Claire."

"Much better. You have a nice voice. Tell me why you like your job."

He took a deep breath. She was an impertinent

10

little chit, but he liked her directness. "I like to drive," he said. "I like taking care of the car. I have a lot of free time."

"To do what?"

"Whatever I like."

"Very well, keep your secrets," she said. "Shall I tell you how I got the scars and get it over with?"

"I wasn't curious, miss—Mary Claire."

"It was a car accident," she said. "I was eleven. My brother Michael was driving. He was killed."

"I'm sorry."

"Thank you. You haven't heard this story? The servants don't gossip about us? The awful DeWinters?"

"No. I never heard the name until today—except in *Rebecca*."

"Oh, you saw the movie?"

"Yes," he said and, warming to her, "The book was better. Hitchcock took some liberties."

"Yes, he did. You read the book too? I couldn't put it down."

"You read—" He stopped, embarrassed.

"In Braille, yes. Do you like to read, then?"

"Yes," he said. He had almost said "more than anything," but he didn't want to give away too much. "Why are the DeWinters awful?"

"My mother ran away to marry my father. My grandfather never forgave her. Then he disowned my brother Phillip when he found out he's...different."

He didn't ask what she meant. "Not much compared to Maxim in *Rebecca*," he said. "Nobody murdered anybody."

"Phillip tried to kill himself, though."

"You're a little hard on brothers," he said before he

thought, and then, horrified, stammered, "Oh, Lord—I'm sorry, miss, I didn't mean to say that."

"I won't tell on you," she said. "You're probably the only person at Westfield Court who's read an entire book."

"Your grandfather has a wonderful library," he objected.

"But have you ever seen him read one? Once they finish school, the St. Jameses don't read. The DeWinters are readers. Impractical, Aunt Edna would say."

"Yes, I suppose she would."

"Oh, I see you don't like my Aunt Edna."

"Are you trying to get me into trouble?"

"No—I promise I won't repeat anything you say to me. Will you do the same?"

"I never repeat anything," he assured her.

"The perfect servant," she said.

"No," he said stiffly. "But I value discretion."

"I'm sorry," she said softly. "I didn't mean to offend you."

"No, you didn't," he said. He might have said more, but they turned into the long, curving drive in front of Westfield Court, and Mr. Lennox came out to greet the visitor.

"We're here?" Mary Claire asked. "Is it as ugly as ever?"

"It's magnificent architecture," he protested. The house had been built in 1834 in the Greek Revival style, modified over the years but still elegant and imposing.

"But terribly gloomy?" she asked.

He didn't answer. He got out and opened the door for her, but Mr. Lennox took it from there. Neil stood by as the butler helped her out of the car and she took his arm.

"Thank you, Vincent," she said, lifting her face questioningly as if she was trying to locate him.

"My pleasure, Miss DeWinter," he said. She smiled, a gentle, warm smile. He understood why her friends called her Sunny.

When he had parked the car, he went back to his room above the garage and finished *The Return of the Native*. The space was small and slightly musty, furnished with only a narrow bed, a plain dresser, a single chair, and a tiny bathroom, but he had more than a hundred books arranged alphabetically on the shelves against the south and west walls. Not much compared to the magnificent collection in the main house, but these were all his, purchased with his own money and with his name neatly lettered inside. He took Daphne du Maurier's *Rebecca* down from the shelf. Perhaps it was time to read it again.

****

On Sunday morning, Mrs. St. James summoned Neil to the drawing room and sourly asked him to take Miss DeWinter to church.

"Yes, ma'am," he said. "The Church of Christ?" He knew where it was but had never been inside.

"The basilica," she said, her mouth twisted in disapproval. The basilica was in Brierly, on the other side of the railway station. "Make sure she gets inside all right. She's blind, you know."

Now you tell me. "Yes, ma'am."

"I don't know which is worst," she grumbled. He didn't think she was talking to him anymore. "Blind, Catholic, and a damned DeWinter." She waved him out of the room as if she had just noticed he was still there.

Mary Claire was waiting at the door when he brought the car around. She descended the steps on her own, using her cane expertly. He got out to help her, and she smiled and said, "Good morning, Mr. Vincent. Or no, you did say I could call you Neil, didn't you?"

"Yes. Good morning, Mary Claire." She smiled again and let him help her into the car. She wore the same dress as at the railway station, or one very like it—plain, simple, and dark. He had not seen her since, but he had heard things about her. Mr. Lennox, who remembered her well from earlier visits, found her overly familiar with the servants. Jane said her clothes were dreadful, but she was sweet, if a little odd. She was kind and generous to everyone and very easy to please. He didn't glance in the rearview mirror as he pulled out on the road, in case she really could feel his gaze on her.

"Did Aunt Edna tell you where I want to go?" she asked.

"She said the basilica."

"Our Lady of Sorrows," she confirmed. "A very gloomy name, isn't it?"

"I suppose it is."

"Aunt Edna doesn't approve," she said. "She doesn't approve of me in general."

"I'm sure that's not true," he said. "How is your grandfather?" He knew only that the end was near.

"He can't speak," she said, "but he squeezed my hand."

He couldn't think of an appropriate response and concentrated on the road.

She was silent all the way to Brierly and then

asked, "Do you go to church?"

"No."

"Why not?"

"That's very personal," he said.

"Is it? I'm sorry. My father is always telling me not to be so nosy. Are we almost there?"

"Almost." Brierly was quieter today, not many people about so early on a Sunday. Quite a few cars were parked in front of the church, but almost everyone was inside. He got out of the car and opened the door for her. "I'll take you in," he said, "and wait out here. Wait for me when the service is over."

"That's not necessary," she said. "I've been here before."

"Mrs. St. James asked me to make sure you got inside," he said.

"What she doesn't know won't hurt her."

"Please let me—"

"Oh, for heaven's sake, Neil, I won't get you fired. Nobody will tell Aunt Edna you let me go in alone." She let go of his arm and unfolded her cane.

He backed off, but he didn't like it. She was very young, very small—not helpless, certainly, but her vulnerability made him uneasy. To be perfectly honest, the church itself made him uneasy. The building was very impressive, Georgian architecture beautifully executed. The bells in the tall, narrow steeple tolled sonorously. He admired beauty, so it should have pleased him, but something about it oppressed him.

Mary Claire went up the steps, using her cane to find her footing, and she did indeed appear to be familiar with the place. At the top of the steps, she was greeted by an elderly woman and took her arm, so he was reassured about her safety and went back to the car to wait. He read for a peaceful but somewhat distracted hour.

When the first of the congregation started spilling out through the heavy, carved doors, he climbed the steps, book still in hand, ready to meet her. He waited while sober people in their Sunday best filed out. She was not among them. Reluctantly, going against the flow, he went inside. It was even more beautiful inside than out. The ceiling was very high, its graceful arches reaching toward heaven. The rose windows had gorgeous stained glass in complex patterns, and the walls were covered with vibrantly colored paintings of saints and angels. The nave was so vast that many times the number of people who had come out would have been required to fill it.

Mary Claire sat alone in a pew near the front. She was the only person still seated, and very few worshippers remained inside. He started toward her, but something in her attitude stopped him. He couldn't see her face, but she sat very still, apparently rapt. He thought she must be praying and didn't want to approach her, so he sat a few rows back on the opposite side of the center aisle. He was very uncomfortable. He opened his book but couldn't concentrate on the words on the page. He liked the beauty of the architecture, but not the silence and the shadows. He didn't believe anything lurked there, but the quality of her quiet absorption awakened a tremor of sensation he couldn't name.

After a few creepy moments, she let out a breath of what sounded like relief, made the sign of the cross, and picked up her cane. He rose immediately and went toward her. Without even turning her head, she asked, "What are you reading?"

"How did you know?" he asked, taking her hand.

"I could hear the pages rustling."

"I'm sorry," he said. "I didn't want to disturb you."

"You didn't," she said. "I'm glad you came in. Isn't it lovely?"

"Yes," he said, suppressing his mixed emotions. "The light coming in through the stained glass makes beautiful patterns on the floor."

"I remember." They went out together, her hand on his arm. As he helped her into the car, she said, "You didn't answer my question. What are you reading?"

"It's called *Thus Spake Zarathustra*," he said.

"Nietzsche?" she said, surprised. "You're reading Nietzsche? I don't know many chauffeurs who read philosophy."

"Do you know many chauffeurs?" he asked.

"No," she said, "and you're a closemouthed bunch. Still, I can't imagine any of them reading *Thus Spake Zarathustra*." He didn't answer, and they were on the road before she asked, "What do you think of it?"

"It's not that interesting to me," he said. "It seems a little obvious. Maybe I should have read it when I was younger."

"No," she said. "It seemed obvious to me too, but maybe it didn't when he wrote it."

"You've read it?" he asked, very surprised. "How old are you?"

"Eighteen." She was young enough to sound proud to be so mature.

"That must be some blind school you go to," he said.

"Yes, a very good blind school. It's called Radcliffe."

Embarrassed and even more impressed, he said, "You're lucky you can afford to go."

"I can't afford it," she said. "I had to get a scholarship. The DeWinters don't have any money. It's another reason Aunt Edna despises us."

"It's not a very good reason, is it? You've had to make your own way, while she's living off inherited wealth. Don't tell her I said so."

"I told you I won't repeat anything you say. She never listens to me anyway. She's only waiting for Grandfather to die so she can send me back where I belong."

"She's been very good to him," he said, trying to be fair. "She's kept the household running very efficiently all these years."

"I think Mr. Lennox has more to do with it than she does. I know I shouldn't be disrespectful to her, though. I will be a good little girl and say please and thank you. Can I ask you a personal question?"

"I can't promise to answer it."

"Fair enough. You asked how old I was. How old are you?"

"Old enough to be your father."

"My father is sixty. Are you sixty?"

"No." Compared to sixty, he wasn't so old. "Thirty-eight," he said.

"Really? I would have guessed younger. You must have read a lot more books than I have." She sounded envious. "Are you married?"

"No. Are you?"

She laughed. "Silly," she said. "Have you ever

been married?"

"No."

"Why not?"

"You ask a lot of questions," he said.

She didn't answer. She was waiting.

Oh, very well... "I was in the army for a long time. I guess I never had the opportunity to meet the kind of woman I would have wanted to marry."

"Were you in the war?"

"Yes."

"Was it terrible?"

"Some of it. Most of the time it was boring."

"*Boring*?"

"Yes," he said. "Nothing to read."

Chapter Two

Austin St. James died peacefully in his sleep on Tuesday morning. Preparations for the funeral at the Church of Christ and the reception at Westfield Court began at once. Jane was short-tempered about the extra work, and Neil was kept busy meeting trains and ferrying visitors. He hadn't seen Mary Claire since Sunday until he heard her cane tap along the driveway. It was none of his business, but he was curious. He went down the stairs from his room above the garage, and she was making her way along the path toward the stables.

She was even more drably dressed than before, in a simple black dress meant to represent deep mourning, but with a longer, fuller skirt than her usual. She heard his footsteps behind her and turned. "Who is it? Vincent?"

"Yes, miss."

She listened, making sure nobody else was nearby, before she said, "Good morning, Neil. I'm going to the stables. Do you want to come with me?"

He fell in beside her but didn't attempt to take her hand. She knew where she was headed, and he had never been inside the stables. "I haven't seen you since Sunday," he said. "I'm sorry about your grandfather."

"Thank you," she said, "but he's in a better place now." He didn't answer, and she turned toward him intently. "You don't believe that?" she asked.

"Not in the same way you do, anyway."

"You don't have to be polite with me," she said. "I like talking to you. You don't talk down to me. I'm tired of people saying stupid, boring things to me."

"I'm sure I can be stupid and boring with the best of them," he said.

She laughed, but in a soft, sad way, suitable to a day of mourning. They went down the path to the stables, and she opened the door before he could prevent her. She felt her way to the nearest stall and held out her hand above the door. The large dark horse housed in it nickered and nosed at her hand. "Hello," she said and reached into her skirt pocket for a small bright-red apple.

Neil stood back and watched. He didn't much care for horses.

"Where is the sorrel?" she asked.

"I don't know anything about horses," he said.

"But you can tell me where the sorrel is, can't you?" Her tone made him feel stupid. *None so blind as he who won't see.*

There was an awkward silence, and then he said, "I don't know. Is it a color?"

"Is it—yes, it's a color, sort of reddish brown. Do you see him?"

He made a quick search. "I think it's the one in the last stall on the right—your right."

"Thank you," she said, but he knew he had lost face. She strode with perfect confidence toward the stall that held what he hoped was the sorrel. He must have guessed right, as she greeted the horse as if they were old friends. "Neil, come here," she said, not as if she were ordering a servant, but with the eagerness of a young girl to an equal, a friend. He approached cautiously. "Take this," she said, offering him an apple. "Hold it out to him."

"Mary Claire," he said, "I—"

"I want you to make friends with him. You'll like him. He's a sweetheart."

"He's a horse. I don't make friends with horses."

"Don't be silly," she said, and to preserve whatever respect she had left for him, he took the apple and held it out. Nothing happened.

"Give me your hand," she said, a bit impatient, as if she could sense his awkwardness or hear the horse's failure to respond. She showed him how to hold the apple on the palm of his hand and offer it to the horse. The sorrel took the apple and whinnied approval. "There, see?" she said. "Isn't he lovely? His name is Thunder, but it's a joke. He's very sweet and gentle. Would you like to ride him?"

"No."

"Come on. It will be fun." She opened the stall door, found the horse's head as if she could see perfectly, and stroked him, murmuring endearments. "Give me your hand," she said again.

"No. This is not my job."

"I didn't suppose it was," she said. "You don't have to come with me. I can go alone."

"Oh, Lord, Mary Claire, please…"

"Are you afraid?" she asked.

"Yes."

She turned toward him, deeply surprised. "Of a horse? You were in a war!"

"I wasn't in the cavalry," he said, "and I knew

what I was supposed to do in the war."

"Oh, I'm sorry," she said. "I didn't mean to embarrass you. I wanted us to be friends."

"We are friends. And I am not getting on that horse."

He did, though. He wanted to at least wait for the stableman, but she insisted she could do it herself. She brushed the sorrel, put a pad on, and lifted the saddle, which looked too heavy for her, onto the horse's wide back. She expertly secured the straps, put the bridle over Thunder's head, and helped Neil mount. She saddled the big dark horse for herself and asked him if the cinch looked tight enough. He didn't have a clue. He had last ridden when he was six years old, and he had been terrified. She mounted effortlessly and sat easily astride the big horse. Only then did he realize that her dress was a riding habit with a divided skirt.

They started down the hill toward the river at an easy walk. It was a beautiful day, and he wished she could see the bright green of the grass and the diamond clarity of the deep blue sky.

"Did you finish *Thus Spake Zarathustra?*" she asked.

"No, I gave up on it," he said. He was humiliated— a quitter and afraid of horses too.

"Good," she said. "I didn't want to talk about Nietzsche. What are you reading now?"

"*Main Street* by Sinclair Lewis."

"Oh, I haven't read that one. I couldn't get into *Babbitt*. Is it any good?"

"Better than *Babbitt*." He would have enjoyed this, casual conversation about books with a bright, young mind on a pretty, peaceful day, if only a large animal were not moving under him.

"Are you all right?" Mary Claire asked.

"Not really."

She stopped her horse, and Thunder obligingly stopped too. "Get off," she said. "We'll walk them." He was almost more afraid to get off than to stay on, but he managed, with a little help—from a skinny little blind girl. He wasn't comfortable walking the horses, either, with Thunder breathing down his neck, but the conversation became even more interesting.

"Why don't you go to church?" she asked.

"I'm an atheist."

"No, you aren't."

"I think I would know."

"You don't believe in God?" Her tone conveyed not shock, but innocent surprise.

"No, I don't."

"I do."

"I know."

"Does that offend you?"

"No, why would it? Does it offend you that I don't?"

She thought about it. "I don't think so, but it is sad. I know God exists. I can feel His presence. I'm sorry you can't."

"You're sorry I don't like horses, too," he said.

She patted her mount's nose and whispered something to him. "But look at the world around you, Neil. It's so beautiful, so complex. The universe is so big—how can you not believe? Atoms, snowflakes, stars—it's all so wonderfully organized and—"

"Beautiful," he prompted.

"How can you not be in awe of it all?" she asked.

"I am. I think anybody who isn't just isn't paying attention. But I don't think it follows that an anthropomorphic god created it all."

"But then, where did it all come from?"

"I don't know. You don't either."

"Yes, I do," she said sweetly. He had to admit her certainty was very attractive. "Do you believe in this big-bang idea?" she asked.

"I'm not a physicist."

"But you must have read about it. So what do you think would have come before it?"

"I don't know. What do you think came before God?"

"Before God?" She sounded amazed, but not offended.

"I don't think the big bang is the answer. I don't think God is the answer."

"For me He is."

"They're both just different ways of asking the question. I don't need an answer. As you said, you have to be in awe, but that's enough."

"Is it?"

"Yes."

She was speechless for a moment. She stood still and rubbed her horse's nose. "You *have* read a lot of books," she said. "I'll have to think about this."

"Don't let me shake your faith," he said. "I do respect it."

"Why, if you don't share it?"

"I'll have to think about that. About how to explain it—I know what I feel."

"Nobody talks to me the way you do," she said. "As if I were grown up and intelligent. I'll miss you when I go home."

"I'll miss you too," he said. He didn't suppose he really would, but she *was* an engaging little creature. "Are you going home right after the funeral?"

"And the reading of the will. Aunt Edna says I have to be there. I've never been to one, have you?"

"Yes, several times."

"Will it be sad?"

"Maybe. The lawyers are usually very businesslike."

"Michael didn't leave a will, and I was too young when my mother died. I guess I was too young when Michael died, too."

"Do you blame him?" he asked.

"Michael? No. I did at first, but I still loved him, so it was easy to forgive him."

"Do you ever think, 'Why me?' "

"No, I don't. Why not me? I don't think it's a punishment from God or anything, if that's what you mean. It was me because I was the one sitting next to Michael, and he was driving too fast. I was lucky I wasn't killed too. He didn't mean to hurt anyone. He was just in a hurry. He was always in a hurry. He had a huge appetite for life."

"And your other brother?"

"Phillip is the best of us. He's a very sweet person. He was seventeen when I was born, and my mother died when I was six, so Phillip practically raised me. He had a terrible time for a while, but he's happy now. He lives in Wisconsin with his friend Ivor."

"You mean he's…"

"Oh, I know," she said. "I know what the Church says, but it's wrong. God made them the way they are.

Love is love."

"I'm glad to hear you're willing to question the Church."

"It's like a very old, cranky lady, set in her ways."

"A bit like your Aunt Edna," he suggested.

"Oh, that's mean," she said, but she smiled. They had reached the river, and she stopped and patted her horse reassuringly.

Neil stopped too, and the sorrel nudged his shoulder. Hesitantly he raised his hand and stroked the long head. Thunder made a soft noise.

"He likes you," Mary Claire said.

As they stood beside the river, he was very conscious of the sunlight sparkling on the water, the color in the leaves of the trees, and the dark shadows of the deeper woods beyond. He had a melancholy sense of the beauty that was denied her.

She smiled, though, and lifted her face to the warmth of the sun. She could enjoy it, and she could hear the river rushing over the rapids, the sigh of the wind, the rustle of branches—pleasures he would have ignored if he had been here alone.

He promised himself to pay more attention to the non-visual beauty in the world—sounds, scents, textures.

"It's lovely here," she said. "Let's sit for a while."

"You'll get grass stains on your dress," he said.

"Now you sound like Aunt Edna."

He glanced around. "I see some rocks downstream a little way," he said. "We could sit there." He took her hand to lead her across the uneven ground, guided her to a safe seat on the smooth, flat rocks, and clumsily tied the horses' reins to a nearby tree. An uneven place in the riverbed created a tiny waterfall close by, and they could hear it splashing. The air was cool and flower-scented, the light diffused by overhanging limbs.

"This is perfect," she said. "This will be our special place. We won't bring anybody else here."

"You sound about twelve," he said.

"I feel about twelve. You're so nice—I wish everybody was like you. Will you come here and think of me when I'm gone?"

"I might if I don't have to ride a horse to do it."

She laughed. "You could probably drive the car down," she said. "I feel like God is listening here—like in a confessional. We can't lie. Promise me you'll always tell me the truth here."

"Are you setting me up for something?" he asked. "One of those nosy questions of yours?"

"Maybe."

"All right, I promise. I'll tell you if it's none of your business, but I haven't lied to you yet, and I won't."

"Especially here," she insisted.

"Anywhere. But especially here, if you like." He did think she sounded twelve—making a secret clubhouse by the river.

"Did you kill anybody in the war?" she asked.

"I knew it," he said. "Right for the jugular. Yes, I do have that on my conscience."

"Will you tell me about it?"

"No, I will not. There, that's the truth."

"Do you have nightmares about it?"

"Not anymore. It was a long time ago." It was, and he hadn't stopped dreaming about it until he came to Westfield Court.

"I still have nightmares about the accident. It's been seven years, and I still wake up crying because I can't find Michael in the dark."

"I'm sorry," he said and put his hand on hers in a comforting gesture.

She was silent for a moment, and then she asked, "Will you do me a favor?"

"If I can."

"Nobody will tell me what the scars look like. I can't look in a mirror. They all say, 'Oh, they're not so bad,' and I can tell from the way they say it that it's a lie. A lot of people won't even talk to me, as if they're embarrassed or repulsed. I know looks don't matter…"

"You're eighteen," he said. "It matters to you."

"But not to you? Will you tell me the truth? If you can't, don't say anything—no lies. Tell me what they look like, exactly what you see." She took off her sunglasses.

He was not embarrassed or repulsed, but he was stricken, horrified. Her eyes were so obviously sightless that it was painful to look at them. The scars that were usually covered were worse than the more visible ones, but her eyes were so much more disturbing that he could truthfully say, "They're not all that bad. It must have hurt like hell, though."

"Yes," she said grimly. "What does 'not that bad' mean? Not as ugly as you expected?"

"Not ugly," he said. "Painful. Sad."

She sighed. "I could have more surgery, but they would still be ugly, and I'd still be blind."

"Not ugly," he repeated.

She put her sunglasses back on. "Can I look at you now?" she asked. "Feel your face with my fingers, I

29

mean?"

"If you like. There's not much to see, I'm afraid." He took her hand so she wouldn't have to grope toward him and put it against his cheek. She leaned forward eagerly and deftly explored his face with both hands, her fingers light and quick against his skin. It humbled him that she was so matter-of-fact about her blindness while he was still resisting the need for reading glasses.

"What color are your eyes?" she asked.

"Gray. Blue-gray."

"Really? I thought you would have dark eyes. You have a dimple," she said, fingering a small indentation above his left eyebrow. "Did you know dimples are caused by overly tight muscles? They're technically defects."

"Thank you," he said. "I'll add that to the list of my defects… Oh, Lord, Mary Claire, what time is it?" It was a rhetorical question—he was already glancing at his wristwatch—but she lifted the hinged glass on hers and touched the hands. "I need to get back," he said. "Take my hand."

"Go ahead," she said. "I'll find my way back and take the horses."

"No, let me—"

"Don't treat me like a cripple," she said impatiently. "Go do what you have to do. I know you don't want to see me anymore. I know you lied about the scars."

"No, I didn't. I swear."

"Oh?" she said coolly. "What do atheists swear by?"

"You are too smart for your own good," he said, "but we'll have to continue this discussion another time. I don't want to get fired." He took her hand and helped her to her feet but had to leave her to find her own way back. She was smart, and she was stubborn, and she was altogether too much for him to handle.

****

Neil was in bed with Jane when he remembered to ask her if Mary Claire had gotten back to the house all right. He had worried that she might have trouble with the knots he had put in the reins or stumble on the rough ground, but he hoped the horses could find the right path.

"She came back before Mrs. St. James knew she was gone. I think she'd been crying—which is natural, I guess. Her grandfather, I mean."

Yes, of course, her grandfather. Or was it because she had trusted Neil and he had lied to her? Had he lied? No, but he hadn't told her the whole truth, either. She was so young and so brave, and she deserved better than he knew how to give. He had never had a friendship like the one developing between them and didn't know how to proceed. They had had only a few conversations, and she would be gone in a few days, and now that her grandfather was gone she would have no reason to return. Still, he wished he had handled things better.

"What are you thinking about?" Jane asked. She sat up and put the pins back in her loosened hair. "The little DeWinter?"

"Mm," he said noncommittally.

"Yes," she said, as if she knew what he meant. "Poor kid. I think I'd kill myself if it happened to me."

"Don't let her hear you say such things."

"No, of course not," she said, not at all offended. "I

know which side my bread is buttered on."

That was Jane—practical and unemotional. She had originally been Janelle, but Mrs. St. James hadn't considered the name suitable, so she had become Jane and never looked back.

Chapter Three

Neil drove the Bentley to the Church of Christ for Austin St. James's funeral. Mrs. St. James sat in the back seat with Mary Claire and Jane, and Mr. Lennox sat up front. Mrs. St. James had kept her niece, neatly dressed in dismal black, close to her in a display of family solidarity, practically dragging her by the arm. He could tell Mary Claire didn't like it, but she went along meekly enough, saying nothing.

He didn't have a chance to speak to her until they got out of the car at the church and Mrs. St. James turned away to speak to another mourner. "Mary Claire," he said softly so her aunt wouldn't hear the presumptuous use of her Christian name.

Before he could say more, she gripped his arm and whispered, "I'm sorry."

"You have nothing to apologize for," he said. "I'm sorry I abandoned you."

She shook her head. "I'm sorry I made you look and then called you a liar. I'm sorry about the atheist thing, too. That was mean."

"Come on," her aunt said impatiently, grabbing the girl's arm. "This is my niece," she said to the woman she had been speaking to, and they moved toward the church.

The building was not as imposing as the basilica, but it had charms of its own. Neil liked the simplicity of it, which was, after all, a reaction against the lavish Catholic style. He sat at the back with the rest of the staff, and Mary Claire was next to her aunt in the front row. The stiffness in the way she held her head had nothing in common with her rapt attention on Sunday.

The congregation stood while the coffin was carried to the front of the church. Mr. Lennox was one of the pallbearers. Neil recognized two of the others but didn't remember their names. He was out of place here. The minister spoke of Austin St. James in general terms, as if they had never met, and intoned words Neil would have found offensive if they hadn't been so familiar: "How say some among you that there is no resurrection of the dead? But if there be no resurrection of the dead, then is Christ not risen, and if Christ be not risen, then is our preaching vain, and your faith is also vain."

The congregation sang "How Great Thou Art." He liked hymns because they were usually so beautifully written, and this one could give him chills when sung well. This congregation sang it automatically, without sentiment, and he wondered if any of them had anything like Mary Claire's simple faith.

The best part of the service came next. Mary Claire stood straight and proud, alone next to the piano, and sang in a clear, sweet soprano, at her grandfather's request:

Softly and tenderly Jesus is calling,
Calling for you and for me;
See, on the portals He's waiting and watching,
Watching for you and for me.

~

Come home, come home,

Ye who are weary, come home;
Earnestly, tenderly, Jesus is calling,
Calling, O sinner, come home!

~

Why should we tarry when Jesus is pleading,
Pleading for you and for me?
Why should we linger and heed not His mercies,
Mercies for you and for me?

~

Come home, come home,
Ye who are weary, come home;
Earnestly, tenderly, Jesus is calling,
Calling, O sinner, come home!

By the time she sat down, there was not a dry eye in the house. Neil told himself it was the beauty of the music and her lovely voice as he blinked back tears. He remembered her saying her grandfather was in a better place. This was what it meant to her—Austin St. James had gone home.

Outside after the service, Neil waited, leaning against the car, a chauffeur again, no longer a mourner, and watched Mary Claire. She stood next to her aunt as people approached to offer condolences. Time after time, they grabbed her hands without warning or failed to identify themselves. She was tired and bewildered, but unfailingly polite.

In the car, she sat silently, calm and dry-eyed, while Mrs. St. James and Jane gossiped about what people had said and what they had worn. He wanted to know what went on in her funny little head. He wanted to tell her how her singing had moved him. He wanted to tell her she was worth a dozen of those other mourners, scars or no scars. If he hadn't been twenty years older than she was, he would have said he had a crush on her.

****

The following morning, Mrs. St. James called Neil into her study. She was in a foul mood. "Vincent," she said in an aggrieved tone. "Miss DeWinter wants to have a picnic, of all things, by the river. I don't know why someone can't walk her down the hill, but no, she wants the car. She can't be left alone. It isn't your job to nursemaid the little brat, but I can't spare anyone—"

"That's fine, ma'am," he said. "I don't mind driving her. I'll make sure she comes to no harm."

She sniffed. "You can drown her, for all I care. They drown blind puppies. That's all, Vincent." Where, he wondered, was yesterday's family feeling?

He brought the car around, and Mary Claire came down the steps carrying a basket. He didn't get out of the car to help her. "Are you mad at me?" she asked as soon as she was settled in the back seat.

"No, of course not. Did you plan this picnic just to talk to me?"

"Maybe. It's a nice day for it, isn't it?"

"Very nice. I wanted to tell you yesterday how much I liked your solo. You have a beautiful voice."

"Thank you," she said. "I was afraid you would think it was creepy."

"It was beautiful. Very moving."

"Some atheist you are," she said.

"I'm also a music lover. What's in the basket?"

"Sandwiches and things. I don't think you're really an atheist."

"If it bothers you, we don't have to talk about it," he said. "Where do you want to go?"

"Our special place. Were you raised as a Christian?"

"My mother was a Quaker. Would it surprise you to know I still consider myself a Christian?"

"No, but then you can't be an atheist."

"Oh, yes, I can. I forgot where this place was—oh, no, it's down there."

She leaned forward, holding onto the seat back, in her eagerness for answers. "Tell me what you meant," she said.

"Okay, but let's stop here and walk the rest of the way. I don't want to get stuck." He parked the car on an angle and set the parking brake to be sure it wouldn't roll down the slope. This time he did open the door for her but let her get out on her own.

"Are you sure you aren't mad at me?" she asked.

"I'm sure. I don't need to help you, do I? You're not a cripple."

"Oh, I see," she said. "Now tell me…"

"Watch your step here," he said. She used her cane and made her way down ahead of him. "A little to your left," he said when she hesitated.

"Stop stalling," she said, feeling her way to a seat on a flat rock.

"I consider myself a Christian," he said. "Meaning a student or follower of Christ—of Jesus, that is, but I don't object to the title. He was a real person, you know, and he had ideas that have changed the course of civilization. I just don't believe he was any more the literal son of God than any of us."

"You take my breath away," she said. "Literally. I can't breathe."

"I think you can handle this, or I wouldn't have

gotten into it. Your faith isn't some little fairy tale that will disappear when the light shines on it, is it?"

"That's probably the nicest thing anybody ever said to me—besides Phillip. Let me think about this for a minute."

"Take your time," he said. He took the basket from her and surveyed what she had brought. Sandwiches of an undetermined variety. Apples. Chocolate chip cookies. Cartons of milk. A child's lunch. The sandwiches were probably peanut butter and jelly. She was a child, and he had no business even talking to her.

"What about the Blessed Virgin?" she asked.

"Not a virgin, obviously. The Catholic Church's version of a goddess. I'm sure she deserves respect, and if it comforts you to pray to another woman, be my guest."

"That's—"

"You don't have to agree with me. You won't go to hell for listening to me—and you did ask."

"So—why are you a Christian?"

"Because… Do you know the most important thing Jesus said?"

"John 3:16," she said. "For God so loved the world as to give his only begotten son that whosoever believeth in him may not perish but may have life everlasting."

"No, not that one," he said. "I have serious objections to that one. I don't think Jesus even said it. No—I don't know chapter and verse like you do, but it's 'The kingdom of God is within you.' "

"Luke 17:21," she said.

"Oh, very good. Do you know what it means?"

"I—tell me what *you* think it means."

"The disciples were anticipating the Second Coming, a literal kingdom of God being established on earth. Jesus said it's here right now—it's within us. It's up to us. We need to make our own heaven on earth, to take care of each other, feed the hungry, do unto others, et cetera. That's Christianity, Mary Claire."

"We can agree on that much," she said. "But what's wrong with John 3:16?"

"Do you believe Jesus died for your sins?"

"Yes."

"Why? Why should anybody have to die for anybody else's sins? Especially yours, as puny as I'm sure they are. According to John 3:16, God sacrificed his son—why? To appease himself? Does that make sense to you? Does it sound like a loving god? Human sacrifice was an acceptable idea when the gospels were written, so maybe it made sense to them. It doesn't to me. I don't believe in human sacrifice, and I don't believe a loving god would condemn those who can't or won't believe."

She was silent.

"Come on. If you believe it, defend it. Give me hell."

She shook her head. "I can't. I have to think about it for a while. You have twenty years on me."

"Fair enough," he said.

"If Jesus didn't say it, why is it in the Bible?" she asked.

"The crucifixion was a crushing blow to early Christianity. I think it was St. Paul who redeemed it by deciding he had died for our sins."

She was silent for a moment, and then she said, "I don't believe you're an atheist. You talk about a loving

God…"

"That's what you believe in, isn't it? I don't. I can be a Christian without believing in ancient fairy tales. Your faith is beautiful, but it has nothing to do with Christianity."

"You think I believe in fairy tales?"

"I don't know. Do you? Nobody knows what you believe except you."

"I believe in God, a loving God. Anyway, you're too nice to be an atheist."

"Not believing in God doesn't automatically lead to depravity."

"No, but…"

"My morality is based on self-respect, not religion."

"What do you mean?"

"Think about it."

She did. "Yes, I see," she said. "I was sorry for what I said to you, but I didn't think God would punish me. I could have gone to Confession, and I know He would have forgiven me, but it made me feel bad about myself. Are you sure you're not mad at me? You told me things that were none of my business, and I was horrible to you."

"It's all right. I have a tough hide."

"I shouldn't have made you lie to me and then blamed you."

"I didn't lie," he said.

"Yes, you did."

"Let's start again," he said. "Take off your sunglasses."

"No." She bit her lip.

"Are you afraid of the truth now?"

"No, I just don't want to. I have a headache. The sun—"

"I'm sorry. Can I do anything to help?"

"Talk to me." She sounded as if she was doing her best to keep a brave front. He was conscious of having failed her, and he still wanted to put it right.

"You don't need to take them off," he said. "I can remember."

"Don't," she said, on the edge of tears.

"They're just scars. I've seen worse."

"In the war! You were shocked. I could tell."

"I was, but not by the scars. Your eyes—"

"My eyes?" She sounded frightened. "Are they horrible?"

"They are heartbreaking," he said. "They must have been beautiful once, and to see someone so young with eyes that are so obviously…"

"Useless?" she guessed.

"Useless," he agreed. "So yes, I was shocked. The scars are nothing. You have a beautiful mind and a beautiful heart, and any idiot could see past the scars."

"Thank you," she said dutifully. "But they're still ugly."

"No, they aren't. They are your red badge of courage."

"Oh, I loved that book. Was it like that—your war?"

"Not very much."

"Why did you leave the army?"

"I lost my taste for it, I guess. Westfield Court is a more peaceful place."

"Except when Aunt Edna is on a rampage. She was furious with me this morning."

"She's under a lot of stress right now. Be patient with her."

"That's very Christian of you," she said. "Anyway, I'll be going home tomorrow. I'll miss talking to you. If I wrote you a letter, would you answer?"

"Probably." He didn't want to ask how she would go about writing it. Did she use a typewriter? Would someone have to read his answer to her? He supposed she would forget to write anyway, once she was back in her own world.

Mary Claire opened her watch and touched the hands. "Are you hungry?" she asked. "We have lots of time—the reading of the will isn't until three. Or am I keeping you from something?"

"I'm not hungry yet," he said, "and you know what you're keeping me from."

"Really? What are you reading? Did you finish *Main Street*?"

"Yes. I think you'd like it. Now I'm reading Jack London."

"Oh, I love Jack London," she said.

"Is there anything you haven't read?" he asked, amused.

"*Main Street*. And all the books you've read about religion—you should make me a list. I'll show you how to use my Braille writer."

"It's not very Catholic of you to encourage me to challenge your faith."

"Maybe not, but it's very Mary Claire DeWinter. I was always a good little girl—I said my prayers and learned my catechism—but it didn't keep me from thinking for myself. God is still there."

"I'm glad," he said. He was. Her faith was part of

her, and he liked her exactly the way she was.

After they had eaten—the sandwiches were tuna and cheese, not peanut butter and jelly—she asked about the reading of the will. "Why do I have to be there?"

"It usually means you're in the will. He left you something. Only the lawyers know what it says, so they make a list of the people who are mentioned and ask them to be present. You don't have to, but it would be respectful. I'll be there too."

"Does that mean you're in the will?"

"I expect so. It won't be anything much, but it's usual to leave some little token to faithful employees."

"Are you a faithful employee?" She was laughing at him.

"I am faith-less, as you very well know. Your grandfather was bedridden for most of the time I've been here, so he can't be very grateful for my service."

"Let's go sit in the car," she suggested. "I want to see what it's like to be a chauffeur."

"By sitting in the car?"

"Sitting in the front with you."

"What funny ideas you have." He let her take his hand and pull him up from the rock. She made her way surefootedly up the bank toward the Bentley. "A little to your right," he prompted. She opened the front passenger door and climbed in. Shaking his head, he took his seat beside her.

She explored the dashboard. "What is this?" she asked.

"The speedometer. You've seen dashboards before."

"When I was a little girl, too young to drive. Let

me sit behind the wheel."

"You are such a child," he said. They changed places.

She put her hands on the wheel and pretended to steer. "Where would you like to go, miss?" she asked in the deepest voice she could manage.

"Home, Vincent," he said, playing along.

She laughed. "I like being a chauffeur. I get to drive and take care of the car and read books all day. What fun." She turned toward him and put her hand on his arm. "Let me drive it for real," she said.

"Absolutely not."

"Just for a minute. I want to know what it's like."

"It's damn scary," he said. "Pardon my language, but it isn't going to happen."

"Please?"

"May I remind you your brother Michael, with two good eyes and a driver's license, managed to kill himself driving a car?" He regretted it as soon as the words were out of his mouth.

"*That* wasn't very Christian," she said.

He gave in, just as he had with the horseback riding. Apparently she could make him do whatever she wanted. She had him wrapped around her little finger. "If you damage this car and get me fired, I will wring your neck," he said. "Keep your foot on the brake, and if I say 'Stop,' step on it immediately. *Immediately*, Mary Claire. No fooling around."

"I'll be good. I promise." She laughed.

"This is not funny," he said. "I must be losing my mind." He turned the key in the ignition. "Okay, here's the gear lever." He put his hand on hers and showed her how to shift into drive. "Step on the gas pedal very lightly," he said.

She stepped down hard, and the car jerked forward.

"Stop!" he yelled.

She turned the wheel, and the car swerved toward the river.

"Stop!" he yelled again.

She braked.

He turned off the engine. He didn't trust himself to speak.

"I'm sorry," she said in a small, contrite voice. "I wanted to see what it was like. Or maybe I wanted to tame the monster that killed Michael."

He couldn't say anything for a moment. "How did it feel?" he asked.

"Scary," she admitted. "Are you angry?"

"Yes. I'm glad you're going home tomorrow."

Chapter Four

The reading of Austin St. James's last will and testament took place in the library. Mr. Prentice, the family attorney, sat at the head of the long table, with Mrs. St. James, Mr. Lennox, the two familiar pallbearers, and Mary Claire seated around it. The rest of the staff, unwilling to brave the damask-covered sofas, sat in chairs arranged in a line against the wall. Everyone was muted, respectful, and sober.

The reading began with small items and minor cash bequests for the servants who hadn't been at Westfield Court long. Based on seniority, Neil should have been among them but wasn't. Jane was next. She was to have her choice of any two pieces of his late wife's jewelry. Mrs. St. James sniffed, and Neil glanced at Jane, who was quite pleased. She loved jewelry, and some very expensive items were included in the collection. He wondered what she had done to deserve them and suspected he knew. Mr. Lennox, who appeared most emotionally affected by his employer's death, received several bequests, some of merely sentimental value, and was obviously most touched by the gift of the old man's finest watch.

Mr. Prentice continued: "To my chauffeur, Mr. Neil Anthony Vincent, who is best qualified to value them, all the books in my personal library."

Neil was thunderstruck, but nobody else reacted

with anything but boredom, except for Mary Claire, who lit up with her sweet, sunny smile. He glanced around the room. Thousands of books were shelved here—the cash value might be more than Jane's inheritance. The monetary value was not what he appreciated, of course. What would he do with them all? Would he be allowed to keep them here? He certainly didn't have enough space in his room above the garage.

He had missed the reading of the gifts to Mr. St. James's friends, the pallbearers, but they looked well satisfied. He tried to pay attention, but his mind was distracted by the shelves full of books, *his* books. He forced himself to listen.

"To my beloved granddaughter, Miss Mary Claire St. James DeWinter, my sole surviving grandchild"—as if poor, disowned Phillip no longer existed—"the house at Westfield Court and all my remaining possessions and assets—" Edna St. James sat very straight in her chair and glared balefully at her niece, and several of the others gasped, but Mr. Prentice was not finished. "Providing only that she fulfill two necessary stipulations. Firstly, that she permit my daughter-in-law, Mrs. Edna Carrington St. James, widow of my beloved son Marcus, to remain in residence at Westfield Court for as long as she lives, and secondly, that she, as a young woman in need of protection and guidance, marry within one year of my death and remain married. If she fails to marry within the stipulated time or is divorced or widowed and fails to remarry within a year, Westfield Court and the entire estate is bequeathed to the State of Massachusetts for whatever purposes it may deem fit."

Everyone stared at Mary Claire. She was so white her scars were more visible in contrast, and Neil half rose from his chair in case she was about to faint.

"Is that even legal?" Mrs. St. James demanded.

"Yes, ma'am," said Mr. Prentice. "I believe it is."

"After all the years I spent managing this house, not to mention his precious Marcus, he's left me at the mercy of this little—" She rose to her feet, bristling with injured dignity, and stalked out of the room.

Jane, bless her heart, went to Mary Claire, put her arm around her, and spoke softly. She nodded, and Jane led her out of the room.

****

Neil was on tenterhooks until Jane came up to his room. "All those books," she said, smiling. "You did well, my friend." She kissed him and started unbuttoning his shirt.

"So did you," he said. "Is Mary Claire all right?"

"I think so. Poor kid. Nobody's going to marry her, of course. I think we'll all be out of a job. I might have to sell my baubles." She shrugged. "Easy come, easy go."

"Don't underestimate her," he said.

"You a little sweet on her?" she asked with her usual nonjudgmental perception.

"Far from it," he said. "Today she wanted to drive the car."

"The naughty girl!" Jane said, delighted. "But you know, love, it's her car now. She can do whatever she wants with it. Just be sure you get out before she drives it off the bridge."

"You're right," he said. "She's now our employer. She's so young…"

"She's what, eighteen? When I was eighteen—"

"Ah, but you were born older than she will ever be," he said and kissed her.

****

The buzz in the servants' hall the next morning was all about their precarious position. The consensus was that Miss DeWinter was now legally in charge, but Mrs. St. James, who had hired them, still acted as if she ran the household and always would. Bets were laid as to whether Miss DeWinter would stand up to her, now or later. Nobody was willing to wager on her marriage prospects.

Neil went back to his room after breakfast and tried to read Jack London, but he was too distracted to concentrate. A fine thing—he had inherited a whole library full of books and simultaneously lost his ability to enjoy them, and all because Austin St. James had left his considerable wealth to a young girl who probably didn't want it.

When he had made sure the car wouldn't be wanted this morning—at least Mrs. St. James said not, and he hadn't been officially told it wasn't her call—he walked down the hill to the river. He avoided the rocks Mary Claire considered their special place and walked upstream toward the thicker woods. It was another pretty day, early spring, warm and still. He remembered his intention to pay more attention to the non-visual and listened for the sounds of flowing water, wind, rustling leaves, birds, and insects.

A peculiar, shrill, chirping sound attracted his attention. The source turned out to be a small brown nest filled with tiny hatchling birds, guarded by a huffy, black-feathered female. He thought at once that he would like Mary Claire to hear them but reminded himself she would have other things on her mind today.

A little wistful—although she would have gone home today anyway—he walked back downstream. A movement up the hill caught his eye, and there, tapping her way toward the river, was the new mistress of Westfield Court. She was in black again, and her hair was brushed and shining.

He stood still where he was and waited for her. "Good morning, Miss DeWinter," he said formally as soon as she was in earshot.

She stopped. "Oh, don't," she said. She was paler than usual, and her mouth was a grim line.

He approached her and asked gently, "Do you have another headache?"

"No," she said. "But I didn't sleep much last night."

"I have something to show you," he said. "Give me your hand."

She hesitated, but she did as he asked.

He led her upstream and stopped under the tree that held the nest. "Do you hear them?" he asked.

"Oh, it's baby birds," she said. "How sweet." She smiled, but without much conviction.

"I'm sorry. I thought you would like them."

"I do," she said. "I just can't feel very much right now. What kind are they?"

"I don't know, but your grandfather has a bird book I could check."

"No, *you* do," she said with smug satisfaction, and then fell silent, her expression bleak.

"Do you want to talk about it?" he asked. "Shall we go sit on the rocks?"

"In our special place." She tucked her hand into the crook of his elbow and let him lead the way.

When they were seated on the rocks, he said, "I gather you're not too thrilled with your inheritance."

"I'm so glad you got the books," she said. "It made me so happy, and then…Aunt Edna is furious, and she was so mean to me this morning. Nobody's ever talked to me like that before. I've tried to be nice to her, but she hates me. It's not my fault. I didn't ask him to do it. I don't want it."

"Walk away, then," he said.

"Walk away?" she said, as if he was a complete idiot. "Let the state have it, you mean? Aunt Edna only has a little money of her own from Uncle Marcus, and she'd have to find another place to live."

"Then she'd better be civil to you."

"Fat chance. Besides, you and Jane and all the rest would lose your jobs. And the horses, Neil—what will happen to the horses?"

"They'll be sold, I suppose."

"I won't even be able to visit Thunder again. And the money—you have no idea what a difference the money could make to my father, and to Phillip and Ivor, and Michael's family. Did I tell you Michael left a widow and a little boy? They don't have any money. None of the DeWinters do."

"It's not your job to take care of all those people," he protested.

"Shouldn't you be on the other side?" she asked. "Shouldn't you be pushing me into this so you can keep your job?"

"You know I don't believe in human sacrifice. I'm on your side."

51

"Am I the sacrifice, then?"

"Only if you want to be. If I were you, I'd just walk away."

"No, you wouldn't. I should fire you, by the way, for letting a stupid blind girl drive *my* car. There's a reason an eye test is required for a driver's license, you know."

"Actually, it was a very intelligent blind girl, and I'm glad she's still with us."

"I can't live like this, though. I want to go home. I want to go back to school. I can't live with that woman, and she won't leave me alone. She won't give me five minutes to think things through. She's planning my whole life for me, and I'd just better like it, because I'm a stupid little ingrate who doesn't deserve to live in her precious house."

"Tell her off. You're in charge now."

"And how scary is that? I don't know anything at all about running a house like this."

"You said yourself Mr. Lennox does most of it."

"But he doesn't manage the money, and she makes the decisions. I'm eighteen. I'm studying English literature—how useful is that in managing an estate? I'm what Grandfather called a young woman in need of—whatever it was. To put it bluntly, a husband. Aunt Edna doesn't intend to waste a second getting that little detail taken care of. She wants a—oh, what is the word? I can't think straight this morning. An alliance, is that what I mean? She wants me to marry somebody from a good family with old money. She has a list of candidates, and I have nothing to say about it. She's going to auction me off to the highest bidder."

"I always thought she would make a good pimp."

"Neil Vincent!"

"I love it when you pretend to be shocked."

"I *am* shocked," she said, but she couldn't suppress a smile. "I guess I won't fire you, after all. You make me feel better."

"Good. Tell me what *you* want."

"I told you. I want to go home."

"Good choice."

"But I can't," she said bleakly.

"So you want the inheritance, and to get it you have to get married. That's a barbaric idea, by the way. I'd bet on your brains and common sense against any rich guy with a silver spoon in his mouth."

"Thank you, but—"

"But you have to get married. You don't have to let your aunt dictate terms, though. Tell her to mind her own business and find your own husband."

"Oh, sure," she said. "Who would marry me?"

"You don't have any candidates of your own in mind? Some Harvard boy, maybe?"

"I'm blind, Neil. I'm ugly. I'm poor—or I was."

"I told you—you're not ugly, and you don't let your blindness slow you down. You're too young to get married, but I think you were a catch even before you inherited."

"You're very kind, but it doesn't help to tell me fairy stories. Nobody will want to marry me except for my money—Grandfather's money. I don't want that. I don't want to—I don't want to get married at all. Why didn't he leave the money to Aunt Edna? *She* wants it."

"I'm sorry," he said. "I shouldn't be trying to advise you. You should call your father and ask his advice. Or your brother."

"My father didn't want me to come here at all," she said. "He won't take money from me if he knows it comes from the St. James family. Phillip—I do need to talk to Phillip."

"Good idea."

"But I know what he'll say, and it doesn't help."

"For what it's worth, my advice is to go back to school and let the state turn Westfield Court into a museum or a library or a school or something. We'll all land on our feet."

"Where will you go?"

"Wherever I can find a job. Mrs. St. James will give me a good reference."

"Don't count on it," she said. "But I will. What will you do with the books?"

"I don't know. Put them in storage maybe."

"I have to do it," she said. "I have to."

"You don't. Have you prayed about this?"

"Yes, of course. Are you mocking me?"

"Never in the world, Mary Claire. I told you I respect your faith. I admire you for it."

"You said you would think about how to explain that to me."

"Do you really want to talk about this now?"

"Better this than Aunt Edna's list of husband material. I still don't believe you're an atheist. There are no atheists in foxholes."

"It turns out that's not true," he said.

"Maybe you'll see a blinding light like St. Paul."

"You know I don't think much of St. Paul. But I think a lot of you, and one of the things I admire about you is your faith. I find it very touching."

"Touching? That means you think I'm naïve."

"No, not naïve. Or maybe a little naïve, but only a little. Okay, try this—you have beautiful, shining black hair, a very attractive hair style. It would be ridiculous on me."

"What a terrible analogy."

"You have a gorgeous singing voice. I wouldn't want to be a soprano, myself…"

"Are you suggesting faith is a feminine quality?"

"No. I think I had a better analogy the other night, but at my age the memory starts to go."

"Not at thirty-eight."

"Probably even sooner. Oh, I know what it was— you'll like this one. I like bridges. There are all kinds, but nearly all of them are beautiful. They are built for strength, but they also have graceful shapes, especially the ones with arches. I've always liked the looks of them, pictures of them. But I don't like to cross them."

"What do you mean? Why?"

"I'm not sure. It isn't fear of heights."

"Did something happen to you on a bridge?"

"Not that I remember."

"There's a bridge between here and Brierly. You drive over it all the time."

"I don't mind in the car. But if I try to walk across it, I feel as if I'm going to start throwing things off it, including myself."

"Don't joke about suicide," she warned.

"I'm not joking. It's a wonderful bridge, too, in both design and function. Here's the analogy. Your faith is a bridge. It's simple and strong, the best kind of bridge. But I can't walk on it. Deep currents flow under it, and I might jump in and drown."

"Can you swim?"

"Yes, but maybe I'm not brave enough."

"Bravo," she said. "That's very pretty. I don't think it's really how you feel, but it was beautifully done. You should write poetry." She put out her hand to find his shoulder and then his cheek and leaned forward to kiss him lightly above his left eyebrow, where she had said he had a dimple. "Thank you," she said, and she rose and went alone up the hill, tapping lightly with her white cane.

****

Neil heard a familiar, light knock at his door, and Jane came in without waiting for a response. "I need to get out of these shoes," she said, slipping them off. "It's been a long day." He kissed her, and she started getting out of more than her shoes. "The little DeWinter is having a hard time," she said.

His nerves crisped. "Can you help?" he asked.

She shrugged. "The old witch is hiring a maid for her, so I won't have much to do with her. Poor kid."

"You should stop calling her that," he said.

"Hm. What's eating you?"

"Nothing. Like you said, a long day."

"Oh, yes, lazy old you with your nose in a book all day. I know what you need."

He did, but he needed something else too, something he couldn't name.

Chapter Five

Neil didn't usually go into the main rooms of Westfield Court unless he was summoned, but after breakfast in the servants' hall on Saturday morning, he went into the library to revel in the books. His books. A treasure trove of words, all his. Books on a variety of subjects, collected over years, decades, in some cases centuries. Books of great intrinsic value and some he suspected had been purchased for the color of their bindings. He could read them all now, without asking for permission. He could sell some of the ones that didn't interest him and use the money for—what? More books.

He took Peterson's *A Field Guide to the Birds* from the shelf and slowly turned the colorful pages, looking for the black-feathered mother of the nestlings.

The door opened, and "the little DeWinter" came in. He was glad to see her, and she looked better than she had the last time, with a little color in her cheeks. "Good morning," he said.

She jumped. "Oh—Neil. I didn't know anybody was here. I'm hiding."

"Shall I go?"

"No. Talk to me. I need somebody to say something to me, anything, without biting my head off."

"Things aren't going so well?"

"I called Phillip last night, and he said I sounded as if I was underwater. That's how I feel, too."

"Jane said you were having a hard time."

"She has been very kind, but now I'm going to have some starched busybody messing with my things. Why can't they understand that I can't find anything if I don't know where it is?" She sounded exasperated.

He almost said, "You poor kid," but suppressed it.

"What are you doing here?" she asked. "Visiting your books?"

"Something like that." He slid the *Field Guide* back on the shelf. He knew she recognized the sound, but she didn't ask what it was—a telling sign.

"I thought this would be a good place to hide, because she knows I can't read any of these books. Of course, she thinks I can't read at all. She thinks I'm stupid. She hates me. She will not leave me alone."

"You'll have to stand up to her sometime," he said.

"I know," she said dismally. "I try, but she doesn't listen. You men are so lucky. People listen to you."

"Nobody listens to servants."

"I do, when they make more sense than other people. Which is pretty much all the time these days."

"Things will calm down," he said.

Footsteps approached in the hall, and Mrs. St. James pushed the door open. "Oh, here you are." She sounded angry. "Why are you in the library, of all places? Oh, Vincent. What are you doing here?"

"The books—" he said.

"What? Oh, the books. Oh. What are you going to do?"

"I don't know. I was just…taking inventory."

"If you take them, the room will be too bare. We'll

have to fill the shelves again. You can't have a library without books. You can leave them here if you want, for the time being, and—come in here whenever you want, of course, to..." She was apparently unable to figure out what people did with books.

"Read them," Mary Claire said.

"Yes, read them," she said. Her eyes narrowed as she glared at her niece. "What are you wearing? Those shoes don't go with that dress at all."

"They're comfortable."

"I'm sure they are," Mrs. St. James said nastily. "Vincent, bring the car around in fifteen minutes. We're going to Brierly."

"No," Mary Claire said.

"Yes. Don't use that tone with me. Go get a sweater. It's cool out."

"I'm fine."

"Get a sweater. Stop acting like a stupid little brat."

"Mrs. St. James," Neil said, with some idea of defending Mary Claire.

"Fifteen minutes, Vincent. That will be all."

He wished he could exchange a glance with Mary Claire, but those large dark lenses hid what should have been the windows to her soul. Instead, he said, "Yes, ma'am...Miss DeWinter," and went out.

****

Neil brought the car around and had to wait another ten minutes before the two women came out, Mrs. St. James almost dragging Mary Claire, who was not wearing a sweater. She pulled away before they got to the car and opened the door herself. They sat as far apart as possible in the back seat and didn't speak a word to each other. As the car started across the bridge,

Mary Claire asked, "Are we on the bridge?" Her aunt stared at her as if she were insane.

"Yes," Neil said. In the rearview mirror, he saw her give him a small, secret smile.

They stopped first at a fashionable dress shop. Mary Claire's expression suggested she was as willing to go inside as he would have been. "Leave the cane in the car," Mrs. St. James said as she got out.

"I need it."

"No, you don't. I won't have you going around Brierly looking like a charity case."

"I still look blind without the cane. I'm *not* a charity case. The cane is part of my independence."

"Will you grow up?" Mrs. Saint James snapped.

"I am grown up. I'm eighteen."

Her aunt sniffed. "Then act like it. Try to behave as if somebody had taught you some manners."

Mary Claire slammed the car door. She took the cane with her but didn't unfold it.

They were inside for a long time. Neil tried to concentrate on his book but kept wondering how he could help her. It was not his place, but she so clearly needed help, and they were friends...weren't they? Could a chauffeur be friends with a reluctant heiress?

She came out alone, using her cane. He got out of the car and said, "Allow me?" She put her small, warm hand in his with a grateful smile and let him assist her into the car.

She put her forehead against the back of his seat and said, "Oh, help. I'm going to strangle her—if she doesn't strangle me first."

"Anything I can do to help?"

She sat up. "Take me to church tomorrow?"

"Of course."

"Will you go in with me this time?"

"I can't sit through a Catholic Mass."

"It can be quite beautiful. You like beauty."

"I would feel like a hypocrite."

"I don't see why."

Before he could answer, the shop door opened, and Mrs. St. James came out, accompanied by a young man with his arms full of packages. "Watch out, here she comes," he said. He got out and helped the clerk stow the packages in the trunk. By the time he got back in the car, Mrs. St. James and Mary Claire were arguing about their next destination, which turned out to be a shoe store.

"I like these shoes," Mary Claire said. "They're comfortable. Nobody looks at my feet anyway."

"I do. They're disgraceful. Are you incapable of behaving like a civilized human being for five minutes at a time? Even Helen Keller learned to fold her napkin."

"Mrs. St. James," Neil said. It was a warning. He was dangerously close to losing his temper and very likely his job.

"That was a despicable thing to say," Mary Claire said.

"Using big words now, are we? Just shut up and try on a few shoes. It won't kill you."

Mary Claire shut up. Reading her expression was difficult, because he received no clues from her eyes, as with most people, but her chin was up, and her lips were pressed together tightly. He was glad he would not have to witness the clash of wills in the shoe store.

On the way home, Mrs. St. James was in a far

better mood, apparently pleased with the success of the shopping expedition. Her niece didn't say a word. He glanced at her when the car started across the bridge, and she smiled again, but not at him. At Westfield Court, he opened the door and helped Mrs. St. James out and then Mary Claire. Her hand lingered in his and she said, "Thank you, Vincent," very sweetly. Before she could unfold her cane, her aunt grabbed her arm and forced her up the steps.

Neil took his feelings out on the car, scrubbing every already-gleaming surface hard enough to be in danger of damaging the finish and then polishing until his wrists and fingers ached. If this continued, he would definitely lose his job long before Mary Claire's year of grace was over.

****

Sunday morning brought rain, and Neil met Mary Claire at the front door with an umbrella. She took his arm with complete confidence and said, "Good morning, Neil."

"Good morning. How are you?"

"Very well," she said. She seemed tired but calm. "She hates it when I go to the basilica, but at least she doesn't want to go with me."

He held the umbrella while she got into the car. As soon as he was back in the front seat, she said, "I have something to tell you, but I want to pray about it first."

"Can we talk about something else?"

"What?"

"I don't know. You're being very mysterious. I hope it's something good."

"No, it isn't," she said grimly. "We could talk about you."

62

"I'd have to wake you when we get to the church."

"What?"

"You'd fall asleep because the subject is so boring. You said you liked my jokes."

"Oh, sorry. I'm a little slow this morning."

"You look very pretty, though."

"Do I?" She was still in mourning, but her black suit had a more stylish cut than usual, and she wore a soft blue blouse, a trim little hat, and a slender gold bracelet. She had pink lipstick on, too, which he didn't think he had seen before. "She wants me to look like a St. James," she said bitterly.

"I like it," he said. "The lipstick is nice, too."

"Jane said it would draw attention away from my eyes."

"She's very smart about such things."

"I like her," she said.

"So do I."

"She likes you too."

"Of course she does. I'm a terrific guy."

"Yes, you are. You should marry her."

"Whoa—that's quite a leap. We're neither of us the marrying kind. I guess you have marriage on your mind right now."

"Don't remind me," she said and changed the subject. "I've been thinking about what you said about John 3:16. It says God *gave* his son to us—maybe just to teach us? The idea that he died for our sins is somewhere else—Corinthians or Romans I think. That was St. Paul, and he said himself that his words didn't necessarily come from God, so you might be right about that part. At least I agree that Paul has a lot to answer for. I still believe in the Resurrection, though."

"I wasn't trying to shake your faith."

"You haven't—you've clarified it. I was getting a little muddled, thinking too much, and you cut right through it. I see now that I don't have to believe the particular teachings of any religion. I have my own faith. I like the Catholic rituals I grew up with, but I don't have to embrace every single tenet. Aunt Edna is a Pauline, but she's no Christian. If you can be a Christian atheist, I can be a non-Pauline Catholic. Right?"

"Right. But I never meant to change your mind about anything. I was just explaining my own position."

"Which has nothing to do with bridges," she said, laughing. "Or maybe you haven't come to the bridge yet, and you'll cross it when you do."

"Or I'll stay on this side where it's safe. I don't share your beliefs, but I'm glad if they give you comfort."

"They are more of a challenge than a comfort," she admitted.

"I respect that too. I'm not up to the challenge. You're right about the Catholic rituals, though. If nothing else, they're aesthetically appealing. Maybe that's why I've always had a fondness for Catholics."

"Including me?"

"Especially you. Jane is Catholic too—did she tell you?"

"No, we didn't discuss religion."

"Not her favorite subject." He parked in front of the church.

"Is it still raining?" she asked.

"Yes. Wait until I come around with the umbrella."

He escorted her up the steps and into the roomy

narthex. "Please come in," she said.

"I'm sorry, I can't. I'll come for you after the service."

She sighed and went alone into the nave.

He sat in the car watching the rain and halfheartedly read *Alice Adams.* As soon as people started coming out, he went inside. Mary Claire was not sitting in the pew, as she had been the first time, but was kneeling with her hands folded and her head bowed. He stopped short and slid into a pew near the back. He felt awkward, embarrassed, and moved beyond words. She was so beautiful in this attitude of prayer.

He had left his book in the car, but he couldn't have read anyway. He couldn't think. He wasn't sure why the shadows of this beautiful place were so oppressive to him. His mother would have found it gaudy, idolatrous, but he had no sense of excess here. He sincerely hoped God was present for Mary Claire.

When she had finished praying, she crossed herself and sat back in the pew, but didn't pick up her cane. "Neil?" she called.

"I'm here," he said and went forward to join her.

"I want to go to Confession," she said. "Do you mind?"

"No, of course not."

"I should have gone before Mass, but I wasn't ready." She touched the hands of her watch. "We have about twenty minutes. Sit down, please."

He sat beside her. "I wouldn't think you could have much on your conscience."

"Oh, you'd be surprised. You should try it sometime. It's better than psychoanalysis."

"It would take far too long for me," he said.

She smiled, and then she put her hands to her eyes, under her sunglasses, and he realized she was crying. She brushed away tears and said, "I'm sorry. I promised myself I wouldn't cry."

"There's no shame in tears, Sunny. Do you want to tell me what's wrong?"

She raised her head, surprised. "That's the first time you've called me that."

"It suits you."

"Not right now," she said, trying to laugh. She took a deep breath. "She wants me to marry The Boy."

"What boy?"

"His name is Drake Whitman. What kind of name is Drake? I can't call him that. I always thought of him as The Boy."

"What do you mean? Who is he?"

"Drake Whitman the Third, actually. Of the Boston Whitmans. Old money, very distinguished family, of which he is not the best example."

"You don't mean Whitman Unlimited—those Whitmans?"

"Yes, those Whitmans. His father was a friend of my grandfather's, and they used to hunt together. They came once when I was here, so I've met him. Aunt Edna thinks it's an advantage because he's already seen me. He's seen my scars, all of them, because he took off my sunglasses. He was mean to me. He was always teasing me, picking on me."

"When was this? How old were you?"

"I was twelve, I think, and he was about eighteen."

"So he would be twenty-four now. Maybe he's matured since then."

"Why doesn't that make me feel better? I can't marry him. I know you don't have to be in love to get married, but shouldn't I at least like him?"

"Maybe you will when you meet him again. You've changed. I'm sure he has too."

"He's stupid," she said. "He doesn't read. I couldn't talk about books with him like I can with you."

"You can talk about other things."

"Like what? Why would he want to marry me? I don't want to marry somebody who only wants the money."

"He doesn't have to marry you for money. The Whitmans have plenty of their own."

"He won't, though, until he inherits. I know it's the money. Why else would he come?"

"He's coming here?"

"Next week. So we can get to know each other and decide if we want to get married. I don't want to get to know him. I know too much already."

"Eighteen-year-old boys can be pretty obnoxious. Twenty-four may be more promising."

"When you were eighteen, would you have thought it was funny to deliberately trip a little blind girl and yank off her sunglasses and tell her how ugly she was?"

"No," he said. When he was eighteen, he had joined the army, much to his pacifist mother's dismay. He had thought he was a man, but he wasn't. He hadn't had much experience with girls until later, and he couldn't remember teasing any of them. He had become a man almost overnight when the killing began. Mary Claire would become a woman when she married. He didn't much like the idea, but it was none of his business.

"Why are you defending him?" she asked.

"I'm not. We'll wait and see what he's like. If he hasn't improved with age, you can say no."

"I don't want to see him."

"I don't blame you, but you can do it. Maybe you'll get a chance to tell him what a jerk he was. If he wants to marry you, and you say no, won't it be just a little bit satisfying?"

She took a deep breath. "But Aunt Edna will—"

"Stand up to her."

"That's easy to say, but I've tried."

"Like you did yesterday? Like a rebellious little girl? Do it like the adult you really are."

"What do you mean? How?"

"Don't be sulky and defiant. Don't argue with her. Tell her what you're going to do and then do it."

"I can't."

"You can. You're as brave as they come."

She shook her head. "I'm not brave."

"Yes, you are. Being blind doesn't make you afraid, does it?"

"Yes, it does, all the time."

"But you—"

"I overcome it. I work hard all the time at overcoming it. How else could I live my life?"

"That, my dear Mary Claire, is the definition of courage. You can do this."

She brushed the last traces of tears from her face. "When I was a little girl, I believed grownups were never afraid of anything."

"We stop being afraid of the monster under the bed," he said. "But we find out there are real monsters out there."

"All my monsters are human. Aunt Edna wants a June wedding."

"What's the rush? You have a year."

"I guess she's afraid he'll get away. I hope he does."

"Did you tell her what he did?"

"Yes, but she never listens. She talks *at* me."

He waited for her in the pew while she went into the confessional. He contemplated his own sins and was very sure he didn't want to confess them to anyone.

She wasn't inside very long. She must have had a much shorter list.

Chapter Six

On Wednesday morning, Neil was summoned to the library—not, as it turned out, by Mrs. St. James, but by Miss DeWinter. "Taking charge, are we?" he asked, pleased.

"Fat chance," she said. "I had to talk to you. What am I going to do?"

"About what?"

"About *this*. Can't you see? Are you blind? Oh, don't laugh." She was almost laughing herself, but she still sounded vexed.

"I'm not. What are you talking about?"

"This pimple. It's enormous. How can I meet The Boy like this? Now you *are* laughing. That's just mean."

"I'm not. I don't see anything." She pointed to her chin. "Oh—that? It might feel enormous, but it's only a tiny little pink spot. I'm sure he won't notice. Why would you care anyway? You don't even like him."

"No, but...You're lying to me."

"I told you I'll never lie to you. I'll tell you what, though—you are too young to think about getting married if you can still get in a panic about a pimple. You should be necking with boys in cars and hanging out at the malt shop."

"You're a big help."

"I'm serious. Ask Jane for something to put on it

and then forget it."

"I'm not supposed to bother her anymore."

"Ask your own maid, then—what's her name?"

"Betty. She treats me like a baby."

"I'll tell you a secret about guys. We're very unobservant." Jane had often complained of that particular failing. "When I came in here, I didn't think, 'Oh, look, a skinny little girl with big sunglasses and a teeny, tiny pink spot on her chin.' I thought, 'Oh, it's Mary Claire. I'm glad to see her.' You always look fine to me because you always look like you. If you change your hairstyle or wear a particularly pretty dress, I may not even notice. You think *you*'re blind..."

"You're awful," she said, "but you do make me feel better." She sighed. "I wish I was like you. I wish I was a man."

"No, you don't. A woman is a very special thing to be."

"You only say that because you haven't tried it."

The door opened. Mary Claire jumped and then braced herself. "Oh, here you are," Mrs. St. James said sourly. Word in the servants' hall was that she was even angrier than usual this morning because an article had appeared in the local newspaper: *St. James Granddaughter to Inherit if She Marries.* "Hiding in the library again? I won't have you bothering Vincent."

"She wasn't—" he began.

"Go wash your face and change your clothes. Put on what Betty has laid out for you."

Mary Claire opened her mouth to speak.

"Don't argue with me. I'm sick of hearing your whiny little voice. We have our work cut out for us making you presentable. The least you could do is cooperate."

Mary Claire, very pale, started again to say something.

"Go," her aunt said sharply. She went. "Annoying little brat," Mrs. St. James said.

He couldn't tell whether she was addressing him or herself. "You might try kindness," he suggested, but of course she wasn't listening.

"Oh, Vincent—was there something about the books?"

"No, ma'am."

"Don't forget Mr. Whitman is coming in on the 2:14. And, Vincent, try to make a good impression."

"Have I failed in that, ma'am?" All his feelings about her treatment of Mary Claire were in the injured dignity of the question.

"No, no, I didn't mean anything, or only that he's an important visitor."

"Yes, ma'am. I'll make sure he's comfortable."

****

The 2:14 train was late. Neil waited with equal parts anticipation and dread. He was curious about Whitman, what he was like, what might be in store for Mary Claire. He was nervous on her behalf and wondered if she would like him to drive The Boy off the bridge.

When the train came in, he got out and stood holding his slate with WHITMAN chalked on it. He didn't have any trouble picking him out. He was tall, well-dressed, clearly a son of privilege. He had a valet with him who carried his luggage and pointed out the sign.

Whitman gave Neil a curt nod but said nothing. He

knew this sort—they treated servants like furniture, as if they were invisible as people, unlike the chatty Miss DeWinter. Neil opened the door for him and helped the valet stow the luggage in the trunk. The suitcases were expensive leather without a scratch or scuff mark. He got back in the car. Nobody said a word. Driving back to Westfield Court, he stole glances in the rearview mirror. The valet, who was likely used to being invisible, had reddish-brown hair and a pleasant expression.

Whitman was a decent-looking young man with an aristocratic nose, a stingy upper lip, and a determined chin. His hair was blond and had been very expertly styled. His cologne gave off a subtle, expensive scent. He didn't look as if he would be cruel enough to torment a blind girl. Perhaps he had only been guilty of immaturity after all. Young boys—granted, usually younger than eighteen—often picked on girls they liked, and Mary Claire was very likeable. Maybe she had taken it more seriously than it was intended. Why would a wealthy young man like this consider the proposal if he didn't remember her with some affection? Neil might have hoped this would work out all right if it weren't for the memory of her tears.

He didn't drive them off the bridge. Mrs. St. James wouldn't have considered it a good first impression, and he had nothing against the valet. When they reached Westfield Court, Mr. Lennox was on hand to greet the distinguished visitor. Neil opened the door for Whitman, who never even glanced at him, and went to help the valet with the luggage. The valet said, "Thank you," and held out his hand. "Lou Fraser."

"Neil Vincent," he said, shaking hands with the

amiable young man. "Welcome to Westfield Court."

He had a sick feeling, knowing Mary Claire was about to meet The Boy with no friend at her side, only her demanding and unaffectionate aunt. He wanted to hold her hand or know Jane was with her—something, anything. Monsters, she had said. The monsters were loose.

****

"He's still stupid," Mary Claire said when next they met. Neil hadn't seen her for days and had heard only that the visit was going smoothly, at least from the point of view of Mrs. St. James and the servants, who were satisfied with the hospitality they were providing. He knew she and The Boy had gone horseback riding, but nothing else. Neil was taking her to church again. With neither Mrs. St. James nor Mr. Lennox anywhere in sight, she had joined him in the front seat, which made conversation easier. Young Whitman, who was nominally Protestant, was sleeping late. "He calls me 'babe,' " she said. "He talks down to me."

"That doesn't sound very promising, but give him a little time. First impressions…"

"What was your first impression of him?"

Not good enough, he thought, but he said, "He was presentable, but he didn't say much. He knows how to dress. He didn't look stupid to me."

"But he is. You said to give him a chance, so I did, and he's still stupid."

"Has he been mean to you?"

"No," she said, but she sounded a little evasive. "He acts like he likes me. I don't like him."

"Don't marry him, then."

"I don't want to marry anyone," she said. After a

moment's thought, she added, "St. Paul says it is better to marry than to be burnt."

"Paul again? The King James version has 'than to burn'—I think 'with passion' was intended. But you don't burn, and you're certainly not going to be burnt in hell, whether you marry or not."

"Neil, will you tell me about sex?"

He almost veered into the wrong lane. "No, Mary Claire. It would be inappropriate."

"Hang inappropriate. I need information. Oh, I don't mean *that*—I know what's supposed to happen. I know the fancy descriptions in novels are silly, romantic drivel—aren't they?"

"Pretty much," he said, "but it can be…" He didn't know what to say. "You shouldn't be talking to me about this. You need to talk to another woman." He would have suggested Jane, but he was a little afraid Jane might use him as an example—of what, he wasn't sure.

"Aunt Edna says I'm just being squeamish. She says it doesn't matter who it is because all men are the same."

"Are all the men you know the same?"

"No, of course not, but she meant…you know…in bed."

"And she would know this how? I don't think she's the right person for you to talk to."

"But she will, and you won't. She says after the honeymoon period, he'll leave me alone, unless he wants a child. Only she didn't say child."

"Brat?" he suggested. "I'm sorry, sweetheart, I'd like to help you with this, but I can't."

"Don't do that," she said. "Don't call me

75

sweetheart like that—it's condescending."

"I'm sorry."

"I know I'm being stupid, but I'm not six."

"You're not being stupid. I'm sorry."

"So you said. Do you believe in fated true love and blah-blah-blah?"

"Not when you put it that way. I believe in love that grows between people who are right for each other."

"I don't understand why you aren't married. I can't marry The Boy. I'm not afraid of him, but I don't want to do anything with him. How can I respect a man who would marry me for the money?"

"Isn't that what you're doing?"

"What?"

"Marrying for money."

That silenced her.

When they arrived at the imposing church building, Mary Claire said, "I don't want to go in."

"Why are we here, then?"

"I don't know."

"Are you feeling ill?"

"No."

He waited. He didn't have to be anywhere else. He would be perfectly happy to sit in silence while she decided what she wanted to do.

"You don't want to go to bed with me, do you?" she asked.

"Mary Claire!"

"Aunt Edna says all men—"

"Why would you listen to her when she treats you so badly? She has said mean things about you to me, and if she would say them to the chauffeur—"

"Are you going to answer my question?"

He took a deep breath. "It's a more complicated question than you imagine. I haven't even considered the possibility, so I guess the answer is no. I'm much too old for you, and you're much too young altogether. I would be...honored if *you* wanted to, but it would be entirely inappropriate and would probably ruin our friendship."

"So you *don't* want to. The Boy is older than I am, too."

"Everybody is older than you are."

She ignored that. "He *does* want to. He doesn't care what it would ruin."

He didn't like the new hardness in her voice. "Has he done something? You said he wasn't mean to you."

"Oh, he was very nice," she said bitterly. "Especially if anybody else was nearby."

"What did he do?"

He wasn't sure she would answer, but finally she said, "He kissed me. I didn't like it. Nobody ever kissed me like that before. It wasn't nice at all. Then he grabbed me." She gestured toward her breasts. "I slapped him," she said.

"Good for you."

"It hurt me more than it did him," she said. She held out her hand so he could see the faint bruise. "My aim wasn't very good."

"And then what?" he asked. He could tell by the set of her mouth that more had happened.

"He laughed. He said I couldn't afford to be so choosy, but he would wait until I came to my senses."

"Don't marry him," he said urgently. "Don't do it, Mary Claire."

"He's probably right," she said. "I don't have to decide while he's here."

"Don't do it, even if you lose Westfield Court. You can do better."

"Can I? Look at me."

"I am looking at you."

She took off her sunglasses. "Now look."

He couldn't think of anything to say. He'd said it all before.

She put them back on. "I'll go in now," she said. "Don't come with me." She opened the door and unfolded her cane and went up the stairs very quickly, hurrying so she wouldn't be late.

****

Drake Whitman was at Westfield Court for a week. Neil drove him to Brierly once and was very glad to be treated like an extension of the car. He didn't want to talk to him or even make eye contact with him. The night before Whitman was scheduled to return to Boston, Neil had a dream about him.

In the dream, Mary Claire married The Boy. On their wedding night, called upon to consummate the union, he brutally assaulted her because, he said, he couldn't get it up. "Who could?" he asked, shrugging. "She's so ugly." Mary Claire, bleeding badly, was whisked away to the hospital, and Neil woke up with his hands clenched together, as if around The Boy's throat. He got out of bed and ran into the bathroom and was thoroughly sick.

He sat on the edge of the bathtub with his head in his hands. Where had such horrible images come from? He had had very little to do with Whitman. Could such a sense of evil have come off him? Was it a reflection of Mary Claire's "squeamishness"? She didn't know enough to have fears as specific as his. Thinking of her as a sexual being at all was frightening—because it would taint their friendship, or because he suspected it wouldn't? His interest in her was fatherly—wasn't it? Or fraternal—he was only three years older than her brother—wasn't it? He took a long, hot shower, and lay awake, unable to stop thinking, unable to sleep.

****

Mrs. St. James summoned Neil to the study. As he approached, he could hear voices. The door was ajar, and a voice he guessed to be Drake Whitman's said, "I'll marry the little blind bitch, but I won't take orders from her or you or anybody else."

He pushed open the door and went in. Mrs. St. James, flushed but very controlled, said, "Oh, Vincent, Mr. Whitman is leaving. Please bring the car around at once. Would you see that he gets his train?"

"Yes, ma'am," he said. He glanced at The Boy. "Mr. Whitman," he said coolly and went out.

He brought the car around, opened the door for Whitman, helped Lou Fraser stow the luggage, and drove to Brierly, all on automatic. At the train station, he and Fraser unloaded the luggage, and Fraser took it into the depot. Neil opened the door for Whitman and closed it carefully behind him. He stepped up to the younger man and took hold of his lapels. Speaking softly enough not to be overheard by anyone on the platform, he said, "You *will* take orders from me. Go home and stay there. If you come back to Westfield Court, I will kill you."

He didn't wait for a reaction. He let go of him and got back in the Bentley. He drove away without checking the rearview mirror. He wasn't stupid enough to assume there would be no consequences. If Mary Claire decided to marry The Boy, he would definitely be fired and without a reference. He couldn't have worked for him anyway. He would have to put the books in storage, if he could afford it, and he would never see Westfield Court or young Miss DeWinter again. Even if she didn't marry him, all Whitman had to do was repeat what he had said to Mrs. St. James—unless Mary Claire was strong enough to resist her. He had made a foolish, melodramatic gesture, unlikely to have any effect. Like Mary Claire's badly aimed slap, the threat would hurt him more than The Boy.

It was also damned satisfying.

Chapter Seven

On Friday, Mary Claire again requested the use of the car to go to the river for a picnic. Neil found himself looking forward to it with very mixed emotions. Something dangerous and out of control had risen in his feelings for her. It was not precisely sexual, not deeply emotional, not something he could define, but it scared the hell out of him. He also felt some degree of shame as a reaction to the high of telling Whitman off, revulsion over the dream, and a depressing sense that his last conversation with her had been a failure, which was entirely his fault. He wanted to help her, and he couldn't.

But when she came out the front door she was the same young girl whose classmates had nicknamed her Sunny, and he greeted her and took her hand to help her into the car. "I missed you," she said.

"I missed you too."

They went down to the river and laughed as they recalled her driving lesson. They went upstream to check on the baby birds—all but one had flown the nest—and then sat on the rocks by the little waterfall to talk and share their picnic lunch.

"We're friends, aren't we?" she asked.

"Yes, we are."

"So you'll always tell me the truth—at least here, in our special place? Always, no matter what happens?"

"I'll try."

"You'll only try?"

"Not only. You ask some very tough questions. I don't always know the truth, but I'll always try to tell it as I see it."

"Fair enough. I'll tell you the truth, too… I'm not going to marry The Boy. I should. I wish I could. But I can't. Does that make me a coward?"

"Not at all. I'm very relieved. He wasn't good enough for you. Have you told your aunt?"

"Yes. She's furious, but she's already hunting for another candidate."

"Did you tell Whitman?"

"I wrote him a letter. A nice letter, I think. I did have a better upbringing than he did."

"Tell me, Sunny, if you don't marry and you lose your inheritance, what will you do? What were you going to do before?"

"I wanted to teach."

"You would be good at that. Why not just do it?"

"I've told you why. I wish everybody was as nice as you are." Her voice was wistful. He took her hand and kissed her palm. She closed her hand at once, as if to keep the kiss safe. "That was sweet," she said. "You're very smart, too."

"This from a girl with a scholarship to Radcliffe."

"We're a very intelligent pair," she said. "We should be able to solve all the problems of the world. What have you been reading?"

"It's a book from your grandfather's library."

"Your library," she said.

"Yes, my library. *Surprised by Joy*, by C.S. Lewis."

"Alluding to Wordsworth?" she asked. He had learned that she appreciated poetry far more than he did.

"Yes. You would like it. He was an atheist who became a Christian." He began explaining Lewis's definition of joy, and she took his hand and leaned against his shoulder.

"John 3:16," she said abruptly.

"What about it?"

"I don't love them enough," she said. "I can't die for their sins. I'm sorry if that sounds blasphemous—I guess it doesn't to you—but I don't want to be a human sacrifice. I thought I could. I talked to Phillip last night, and everybody needs money. My father has been ill again, and…last night and this morning I thought I should stop being so stupid about something all women have to do. I should agree to marry the next candidate Aunt Edna comes up with, whoever he is. Not The Boy. I just couldn't. But I thought I could with someone else—anyone else, really. What does it matter? It's not that big a deal, right? All men are the same—except you."

"I'm exactly like all other men," he said. "Except—except you've gotten to know me, and we're friends." He had started to say something else, something that scared him. "If you got to know him—"

"That's what I thought. I'm good at getting along with people. I could be civil even if I didn't like him very much, and I could do—what I had to do, and having a baby might be fun. I like babies. But, Neil, I…I can't. I want to help everybody, but I can't go to bed with some awful boy who doesn't think I'm worth loving."

"Thank God—and don't start. It's only an expression. You are most definitely worth loving, and someday the right man will realize that. He'll look past those big sunglasses and those unimportant scars and see what a pretty girl you are. You have a beautiful smile."

He couldn't remember ever before complimenting a woman without mentioning her eyes. Jane's were dark brown and showed every mood. "You are a terrific young person in your own right, much more valuable than your grandfather's fortune. Any number of lucky young men will fall in love with you, and you with them. Wait for the right one."

She turned toward him and reached for her sunglasses as if she were going to take them off, but she didn't. "In some ways you're blinder than I am," she said cryptically. There was an edge to her voice.

He studied her, wondering what he had missed. She hadn't changed her hairstyle, and her dress was like the ones she had worn in the beginning, not the stylish outfits meant to appeal to The Boy. She wore her favorite comfortable shoes, in spite of her aunt's efforts. Was she talking about the scars again? Or his lack of faith? "I did tell you I'm not very observant," he said.

"Yes, you did." He still thought he had overlooked something, but she changed the subject and talked about going back to Radcliffe. She missed school and her friends, and she had lost a semester and would have to talk to the scholarship office.

So she really had decided to give up, to leave Westfield Court. He wanted to be happy for her, not to feel selfishly that she was ruining what had been a very cushy position for him. He had valued the peace and stability of this place after so much army life, and of course he would miss her. Would she really write to him? If only he could find a way to keep her here without forcing her to make an unwilling sacrifice…

"Oh, Lord, Mary Claire," he said. "We've been looking at this the wrong way."

"What do you mean? Looking at what?"

"Your grandfather's will says you have to marry to inherit. You were planning a marriage of convenience, and your aunt tried to make it a marriage of *her* convenience. What you need is a marriage of *your* convenience."

"I told you I don't want to do that anymore."

"You need someone to marry you for the purposes of the will, in name only. Think about it. Your grandfather didn't say you have to consummate the marriage or solemnize it in a church. He wanted your husband to help you manage your fortune, but the will doesn't say he has to. Find someone who will agree to marry you on paper and won't try to control you or your money."

"Nobody would agree to that," she said. "What would be in it for him?"

"You could compensate him, give him an allowance or a settlement. A scholarship—find a Harvard boy who needs financial aid."

"The things you say always sound logical," she said, "or maybe I *am* naïve. But everyone else would think it was insane. The Boy was willing to marry me because of the money and because he wanted to go to bed with me. Nobody's going to do it for tuition. In name only? He couldn't marry anybody else. Who would do that? I wouldn't. Think about it. Would you?"

It took him about ten seconds. "Yes, Mary Claire. I would."

****

"Are you crazy?" Jane asked. "I thought she was going to marry the Whitman boy. He's a looker, real style."

"She wouldn't care how he looked," Neil reminded her. "He would have used her, Jane, her money and her body, and given her nothing in return, not even respect."

"But that's what rich people do, love. Yes, they use people, why not? Even billionaires pimp their daughters for business mergers. It's always been that way."

"Nobody's going to do it to Mary Claire," he said.

"You are sweet on her, aren't you?"

"Maybe, but this isn't about my feelings. It's a business proposition."

"You're almost old enough to be her father."

"It will be only on paper. To secure her inheritance, nothing else."

"So, what do you get out of it?"

"For starters, you and I get to keep our jobs."

"It's only a job. There are other jobs… Maybe I wouldn't have to sell my jewelry?"

He had known Jane would warm up to the idea.

****

Mary Claire was still uncertain. "I know it's legal, but is it right?" she asked. "It seems wrong. Wouldn't it be a sin?"

"It was a sin to require it of you in the first place," Neil said. "Nobody will blame you if you make the best of it. This is a legal matter, not a religious one. We won't do it in the basilica, so you won't be married in the eyes of the Church. If you like, we can take all references to God out of the service."

"I suppose it's what *you* would prefer," she said.

"No, I have no objection to the words, if you don't mind that it would be only lip service from me. Either way would be fine."

"What if you fall in love with somebody else and want to get married?"

"I don't think it's very likely at this point, but if it happens, I'll tell you right away, and we'll get an annulment, and you'll have a year to find someone else. I'll help you. And if *you* fall in love…"

"Oh, sure, I'll hire a manager to handle my affairs and go back to Radcliffe and go to school dances—Oh, sorry I stepped on your feet. I am blind, you know, and by the way, I'm married."

"In name only. You can get an annulment immediately if the marriage hasn't been consummated."

"An annulment means a marriage never existed. Are you sure it won't invalidate the inheritance?"

"No, but we'll ask Mr. Prentice about it."

"Will Aunt Edna let me talk to him?"

"You're an adult. You don't need her permission. Do you want me to call him for you?"

****

Mary Claire's first test of wills with her aunt, acting on Neil's advice to behave like the adult she was, came when she told Mrs. St. James she could either dismiss Betty or take her as her own maid, as she had decided she preferred Jane for herself. She chose to confront her in the library, where it was reasonable for Neil to be present for moral support.

"I hired her," Mrs. St. James said. "I'll decide what

her duties will be, and I won't tolerate you speaking to me in that tone of voice."

"I'm sorry if you didn't like my tone," Mary Claire said. "She will be working for me." She left the room without another word, satisfied that Jane would attend to her again, far better than Betty had.

Neil did call Mr. Prentice, who was a little unclear as to why the chauffeur was making an appointment for Miss DeWinter, but he met them in his office instead of coming to the house as he had always done for the Westgate Court family. Mrs. St. James was under the impression that Mary Claire was going to the dentist and asked Neil to escort her inside so she didn't have to use "that tacky white cane."

Mr. Prentice was of the opinion that they would be considered to have been legally married up to the time of the annulment, but it would be wise to contract the second marriage immediately instead of counting on a new grace period. Mary Claire was frankly amazed that he could calmly discuss the legalities of such a far-fetched plan and even more when he assured her this discussion would be covered by attorney-client privilege and could not be disclosed to Mrs. St. James. Mr. Prentice helped them draft a formal agreement, which Mary Claire said was unnecessary. "I trust you," she told Neil.

"I know you do," he said, "but you shouldn't."

The agreement specified he would have no conjugal rights, no rights of inheritance, and would not be allowed to control any of her assets. She insisted on a clause that assured he would have the right to advise her.

"As long as it doesn't say you have to *take* my

advice," he said.

Afterward, in the car, she was still worried about the morality of the whole arrangement. "I don't think it's right for you to do this for me," she said. "You should at least get a share of the money."

"My present salary is sufficient," he said.

"You can't still be the chauffeur," she protested.

"Yes, I can. I like things as they are, and if you fire me, I'll divorce you. It's only a piece of paper. It won't change anything."

"Will you at least sleep in the house?"

"There's nothing wrong with the room above the garage."

"Except if Aunt Edna doesn't believe we're really married, she'll…"

"It doesn't matter what she believes."

"It does if I have to deal with her every day. Just until I go back to school in the fall. You could have the room next to mine. It has a window seat and bookshelves."

"Well, we'll try it," he said, with no intention of moving. She was still upset, so he asked, "Is something else on your mind?"

"What will you do about…your private life?"

He knew what she meant, but he didn't answer.

"What you do now, I guess," she said, "but…discreetly?"

"Always," he said.

"The perfect servant," she said. She was probably joking to cover her embarrassment, but it annoyed him enough to want to pay her back.

"And you can do whatever you do now," he said.

She turned very pink, and her scars stood out more

than ever.

He was immediately contrite, but said only, "Discreetly, of course."

****

Jane fell in with the scheme almost at once. She had hoped for a lavish society Whitman-DeWinter wedding, but the secrecy of this one appealed to her sense of drama. While Mrs. St. James consulted with Mr. Lennox in the study, the three conspirators were in Mary Claire's room making wedding plans. The ceremony was to take place in the local Registry Office on Monday morning. Mary Claire, covering all her bases, wanted to go to Confession and take Holy Communion the day before. Jane would be their sole witness. They considered possible excuses to give to Mrs. St. James, but Mary Claire, finally beginning to find her own authority, rehearsed a calm, dignified, "It's none of your concern."

"What shall I wear?" she asked.

"White would be appropriate," Jane said, "but you might want to save it for your real wedding."

"Do I have anything pretty?"

Jane searched the closet, and Neil said, "I like her in blue," remembering the blouse her aunt had bought for her. Mary Claire had never been more appealing, more touchingly young, than now, a little girl who wanted to be pretty for her sham wedding.

"Wait a minute," Jane said, turning on him. "You—out."

"Why?" Mary Claire asked. "We're still making plans."

"I was talking to Neil. He isn't allowed to see what you're going to wear."

"That's ridiculous," he said. "I'll see her before the ceremony in any case. Besides, it's only a—"

"It's a wedding. Out."

He went out.

****

On Monday morning, Neil brought the car around and waited, a little less patiently than usual, until Jane and Mary Claire came out the front door. The morning was cool and misty, and the bride wore a long coat, which kept her dress a secret from him after all. She and Jane, happy conspirators, smiled and whispered as they turned up the drive and along the river road. When they reached the bridge, Mary Clare said, "Did he tell you he's afraid of bridges?"

Jane laughed. "No, of course not. I don't think he's afraid of anything…except maybe having nothing to read." She seemed to have dismissed the idea, but he glanced in the rearview mirror and saw her expression turn thoughtful. He knew exactly what his transgression had been. He had told Mary Claire a secret he had never told Jane, who had known him longer and more intimately. The intellectual nature of their friendship was something Jane had never fully grasped. She was jealous, and it wasn't because he was going to stand up in a Registry Office with Mary Claire.

He waited inside while she took off her coat, so his first view of her in her wedding dress was when she walked up to him in front of the clerk, holding a small bouquet of white flowers and a rosary. She looked very young and very sweet in a tea-length blue gown.

The little ceremony was an odd one, conducted without frills in a nearly empty room. They had chosen to leave all the religious references in the service but had toned down or removed every allusion to love or permanence, so Neil almost doubted the clerk's declaration that, "You have consented together to be bound to one another in lawful marriage."

When all the words had been said, Neil put his hands on Mary Claire's shoulders and gave her a token kiss on the cheek. Jane apparently didn't mind that.

The thing was done, and they headed safely home, somewhat elated because they had carried off their scheme without a hitch. Neil and Jane chatted casually, but Mary Claire was very quiet. He knew what she was thinking about—their reception by her Aunt Edna. She was working very hard to break the habit of submission to that fierce, authoritative woman, but it wasn't easy for her.

They didn't have to wait long. Mrs. St. James met them in the entryway. Jane had let something slip to one of the younger servants, and word had gotten back to their mistress that Miss DeWinter had gone to town to get married. She stared at Mary Claire in her pretty blue dress, holding her bouquet and rosary, and then turned to Jane. "You're fired," she said.

"No, she isn't," Mary Claire said. "I pay her salary now."

Mrs. St. James flushed. "Tell me it's not true," she demanded.

"It is true," Mary Claire said tremulously.

"You're married? To whom?"

Neil stepped forward.

Mrs. St. James glared at him as if she didn't understand why he was there. She glanced beyond him for another possibility. "Vincent?" she shrilled. "The chauffeur? You married the chauffeur?"

"No. I married my friend Neil."

"Neil Vincent? You refused to marry Drake Whitman and married Neil bloody Vincent? You goddamned little idiot."

"This is my house. I won't have blasphemy in my house, and I won't have disrespect for my husband."

"Your *husband*? The chauffeur!"

"Shut up! Shut your disrespectful mouth or get out of *my* house." He had never seen her so angry. Mrs. St. James probably hadn't either. She stomped down the hall and slammed at least two doors on the way to her study.

"That was terrific," Jane said, but Mary Claire burst into tears and sought refuge in Neil's arms.

"I hate it when people yell," she sobbed, "and this time it was me."

"But you stood up for yourself and for me as well. I'm very proud of you."

"I'm proud of myself too," she said, "but it still feels terrible."

"First times are always hard," he said and met Jane's eyes over Mary Claire's head. She had not missed how willingly the girl had gone into his arms or how tenderly he held her.

Chapter Eight

Neil was reading one of the newer books from his inherited collection, *Catch-22* by Joseph Heller, in the room above the garage. He had been sleeping in the house, in the room with the window seat and a view of the river, but he didn't sleep very well there, and preferred to spend most of his time in this more familiar space.

Mary Claire had also prevailed upon him to join her and her aunt for meals in the large formal dining room, which he found very uncomfortable. This was not what he had agreed to, but she had said, "Just until fall," and she had always had a way of getting him to do what she wanted. If eating at the long table with the two women was awkward for him, the situation was positively galling for Mrs. St. James. He suspected Mary Claire wanted him to act as a buffer, but the main result was that icy silence often prevailed. Mr. Lennox was frankly scandalized, and Neil was no longer sure of his status in the servants' hall.

He was already having trouble concentrating on Heller's circular narrative when there was a brisk knock at the door. Jane stood on the landing, uncharacteristically waiting for him to answer. "I wasn't sure if I was welcome here since you married up," she said.

"Don't say things like that," he said, but mildly. He

kissed her.

"That did feel like a welcome," she said.

"Nothing has changed between us."

"What exactly *is* between us?" she asked.

"I don't know," he said, "but I think I like it."

"I kind of thought you did. Nothing in it for me, though, is there?"

"How about this?" he asked, putting his arms around her.

Later, while she arranged her hair at the tiny mirror above the chest of drawers, she said, "You're really not sleeping with her?"

"She's not ready to sleep with anyone. That's the whole point. If she was, she would have married Whitman or somebody like him."

"And when she is ready?"

"When she is, I assume she will, and we'll get an annulment."

"What if it's you she wants to sleep with?"

"As you so kindly pointed out, I'm old enough to be her father."

"I think that's beside the point."

"Which is?"

"The little DeWinter is sweet on you."

"Technically, she's the little Vincent now, and we're friends. We talk about books and religion."

"I bet."

"This isn't like you," he said.

"Oh, how would you know?" she asked and left without the usual goodbye kiss.

****

The next day, Neil happened to come out of his new bedroom just as Jane turned the corner with an armful of towels for Mary Claire. "Good morning, sir," she said cheekily and smiled, but she followed it with, "How's Lolita today?"

"That isn't funny," he said. "If you mean Mary Claire, I haven't seen her since dinner last night."

"Why not? Did you run out of books to discuss?"

"Do you and I need to talk about something?"

The door of Mary Claire's bedroom opened. "Who is it?" she asked.

"It's Jane—and your dear husband."

Mary Claire's face lit up. "Good morning, Neil," she said.

"Good morning to you too," Jane said sourly and brushed past her with the towels.

"Jane?" She turned, confused. "Is something wrong?"

"It's all right," Neil told her. "Are you going to breakfast?" He took her hand and placed it on his arm.

They entered the dining room together for the first time. Mrs. St. James was seated at the head of the table and gave them a speculative onceover. He hadn't thought she suspected the marriage was a sham and wouldn't have cared if she did, but it mattered to Mary Claire. He was glad if this bolstered the illusion, but the illusion was apparently painful to Jane.

****

"But I never promised you anything," Neil said to Jane in the room above the garage after lunch. Mary Claire was at the stables. "We never had rules or promises or any kind of commitment. That's the way you wanted it. You said you weren't the marrying kind."

"So did you, and here you are—"

"I'm not married to her. We're not really married. It's only a piece of paper. If you wanted a piece of paper, you should have said so a long time ago."

"It's not about a piece of paper," she said. "It's about love."

"Did I ever say I loved you?"

"No," she said. "Do you?"

He couldn't answer. He didn't know the answer.

"Message received," she said.

"You never said you loved me, either," he said.

"No," she said, "but you knew I did." She turned toward the door.

"I'm not in love with her."

"That's what you think," she said and went out and slammed the door.

He immediately opened it, and she was still on the steps, composing herself before returning to the house. "I could say I love you," he told her, "if I had any idea what it meant. I don't remember the last time I lived in one place this long. I married Mary Claire to save your job as much as mine. You are important to me. I don't want things to change between us. If that isn't enough, I'm sorry."

"You should be sorry," she said, but she kissed him.

****

A week later, Jane was sitting on Neil's bed, having just gotten out of her slip, and he was unbuttoning his shirt, when they heard the familiar tap, tap, tap of a cane on the stairs. "Mother of God," she said. He put a finger to his lips, and she covered her mouth with her hand. There was a tentative knock at the door. He glanced at Jane, who was silently putting her slip back on—as if it mattered—and opened the door.

"Mary Claire!"

"Is it all right if I come in?" she asked, smiling. "I've never been in here."

"You don't have to come here," he said. "You can always ring if you need me."

"As if you were a servant?" she asked.

"That's the general idea." He didn't know what to say to her.

"I just—oh!" She stiffened and turned her head toward the bed. She knew someone else was in the room. "I'm sorry," she said. "I won't come here again. You deserve your privacy." She turned to go and ran into the edge of the door, apparently disoriented. Neil took her arm and led her outside. He closed the door. "Please forgive me," she said.

"It's all right. Did you need something?"

"The car—no, it can wait." She put her hand out and took hold of his shirt, her fingers searching for a button. Had she already known it was unbuttoned? She flushed with embarrassment. "I'm sorry," she said again and fled down the stairs. He started after her, fearful she would stumble in her haste, but she made her way safely back to the house.

****

Neil detected no change in Mary Claire's attitude or behavior, but when he encountered Jane in the hall she said, "I think she knows it was me."

"How do you know?"

"She hasn't been unkind or anything, just a little cool. We were friends, and now we aren't."

"She'll get over it," he said callously. "It's none of her business." He was not used to this resentment toward Mary Claire. She was not really his wife, and he didn't like feeling as if he had cheated on her. What right did she have to judge Jane?

****

A few nights later, Neil awoke in the still unfamiliar bedroom with the sense that something was out of place. He had a soldier's instinct, a little dulled of late, to awaken alert to possible danger. He stilled his breathing to listen. No, nothing dangerous lurked in the room, no intruder, no fire, nothing sneaking up on him, only an odd, repetitive sound in the near distance.

More curious than concerned, he got out of bed and opened the door. The sound was coming from the room next door, Mary Claire's bedroom. She was crying.

None of my business, he thought. She's entitled to her tears. He was conscious now of the change in their relationship since the wedding. The innocent, intellectual friendship had been a little strained by the new circumstances—sleeping in the house, eating in the dining room, pretending to be what he was not. She had unintentionally come between him and Jane, muddling an arrangement that had been so uncomplicated. He missed the early feeling between them, the pleasure of engaging her bright, young mind, the innocent little trysts at the river—the driving lesson, the bird's nest, the religious and literary discussions, her pleasure in his friendship, her tears, and her courage.

He tried the doorknob. It was unlocked, and he opened the door. She was sobbing. "Mary Claire?" he said. "It's Neil." She stopped crying, but her breath came in soft little hiccups of sound. "Are you ill?" he asked. "Do you want me to get someone? Dr. Young? Jane? Your aunt?"

"No," she said in a small, tear-choked voice. He hesitated and then went into the room. It was completely dark, and at first he couldn't see anything. Guided by her breathing, he went toward the bed. He could barely make out a vague shape, black against blacker. The night was warm, and she had thrown off the covers—he almost stumbled over them. He reached to pull the sheet up, and his hand brushed her hip. She was wearing nothing at all.

"Sunny?" he said, sitting on the edge of the bed. He touched her cheek and the edge of the scarring around her eyes. It was only skin of a different texture and not ugly or repulsive at all. She didn't say anything, but her breathing had steadied. He brushed away tears, kissed her cheek, and then, experimentally, her slightly parted lips. They were soft and sweet.

In the darkness he was blind, and she was beautiful, and nothing mattered except that they were together.

Chapter Nine

In the morning, back in the room with the window seat, Neil was filled with regret, not so much for what had happened as for how it would change his relationship with Mary Claire. At the very least they would face awkwardness, embarrassment. Would she believe he had taken advantage of her innocence, betrayed her trust, and ruined her chances for an uncomplicated annulment? They were "bound to one another in lawful marriage," but she had another piece of paper, the prenuptial agreement, which stated that he had no conjugal rights. What he had done was arguably rape. But he had not asserted his rights. He had made love to a lovely and apparently willing young woman.

She had been willing, hadn't she? He thought so, but the world was full of rapists and child molesters who believed their victims were eager participants. He had not been able to see her expression—and it was always like that for her. She could never see his face, never guess his intentions. He hadn't asked for permission before he kissed her, touched her, made love to her. He was like everyone else, forgetting her blindness and startling her with sudden movements. Had Whitman been rough with her, or merely unexpected? Would she now class Neil with The Boy? He had tried to be gentle—if The Boy had been gentler, would she now be married to him, subject to his contempt and verbal abuse? She had said nobody had ever kissed her "like that"—like what? At all?

Last night he had been certain she was willing, but she might instead have been afraid to resist, too frightened to cry out. Had he imagined the complicity implied by their shared silence? She had been soft and yielding, and she had clung to him and responded to his kisses, hadn't she? Yes, and afterward she had turned away from him to lie curled up, not crying, but not replying when he spoke to her. *Oh, Mary Claire, I'm sorry.*

He was old enough to know better, old enough to be her father. What had he been thinking? They had often spoken as if they were equals, contemporaries, but they weren't. If anything, he was even older now—the sense of having let her down had aged him. A twenty-year age difference was not unheard of, of course. His father had been far older than his mother—and had left her a young widow.

The memory of Jane's *Lolita* reference still stung. It wasn't that bad—Mary Claire was eighteen, not twelve, legally a woman, old enough to consent, but a young eighteen, not yet ready for love. He had thought earlier that she would become a woman when she married—had she? Or was she still a little girl, a vulnerable little blind girl who had been betrayed, hurt, exploited, violated by a man she trusted above all others?

If she did feel wronged, who would she complain to? Not to her best friend at Westfield Court, because that was—had been—him. Not to her aunt, who would have wanted an annulment if she had been sure the marriage was a sham, but who would have had no sympathy for complaints of its consummation. *I told you they're all the same. What did you expect?* Mary Claire had said he was not like other men, and he had told her he was exactly like other men, except...had he been about to say, "except that I love you"?

Yes.

Would she tell Jane? The possibility made him squirm. He had betrayed Jane, too, and she deserved better. If she found out—*when* she found out, because she surely would—she would give him such hell. Or would Mary Claire tell the lawyer, Mr. Prentice, that he had violated the agreement? What would be the legal consequences?

Why was he even considering possible consequences to himself when he should think only of her? Why had he taken the risk? Why had he believed, even in the heat of the moment, that it was in any way natural, right, or somehow inevitable? If he had wanted to comfort her, words would have been more effective. There could be comfort in making love, but surely not for a girl like her, an innocent young virgin. She had a woman's body, but she was still a girl.

A voice in his head, surprisingly like Jane's, rebuked him: *Neil Vincent, you dirty old man.* He had told Mary Claire she was special, deserving of love, and shouldn't settle for less, only to let her give herself to a thirty-eight-year-old ex-soldier, a commitment-shy chauffeur who wanted nothing more than to escape into the world of books. He deserved worse punishment than any the world could give him. Perhaps this was what the idea of hell was for. Would she hate him forever? Now that the dreaded loss of her precious virginity was behind her, would she be more or less willing to marry someone like The Boy? He knew he had reduced her value on the marriage market—no longer a virgin, a divorcée, a foolish girl who had married her chauffeur.

He showered and dressed, trying not to think too much, but filled with a deep, sickening apprehension. When he went out into the hall, he could hear the shower next door and knew she was up. He resisted the temptation to try her door. If it was now forever locked against him, he didn't want to know.

He went downstairs. Mrs. St. James was ahead of him in the dining room. "Good morning," he said and received a stiff nod in reply. She hardly ever spoke to him anymore, and when she did she never used his name. He still functioned as her chauffeur, but she could no longer call him "Vincent" in her familiar, bossy tone, and "Neil" or "Mr. Vincent" would have choked her.

Hot dishes were laid out on the sideboard—bacon, eggs, hash browns, oatmeal, anything he could want. He didn't want anything. Mrs. St. James, who had been toying with her poached egg since he entered the room, cleared her throat. "I'll need the car today," she said and with evident reluctance, "if it's convenient."

"You'll have to ask Mary Claire," he said. A shiver of feeling went through him when he said her name. He filled a plate without interest and sat down to eat. He had brought a book—*The Last Temptation of Christ* by Nikos Kazantzakis—as he often did. Mrs. St. James thought it was rude, but he was sure she was relieved, as well.

He had been enjoying the book very much, but this morning he couldn't concentrate. He read the same page several times without absorbing a single word. Time stretched out forever—how could Mary Claire possibly take this long to shower and dress? Would she come down at all? Was she avoiding him?

After what felt like hours, her cane tapped along the hall, and she pushed open the door. He rose and stared at her. She looked as she always did. No, she didn't—there was a difference. Not in her, in him. She was beautiful to him now, her face as well as her gentle, kind spirit. She had an exquisite little chin, a slight dimple beside her mouth, a perfect nose. Even her scars were beautiful, and the dark lenses lent an air of mystery. Her modest dress, barely hinting at breasts and hips, only added to her allure. "Good morning," he managed to say. She had taken his breath away.

"Good morning," she said. She sounded perfectly natural, calm and cheerful. He couldn't detect even the slight coolness Jane had complained of.

"Good morning," Mrs. St. James said grumpily. "I need the car."

"Good morning, Aunt Edna," Mary Claire said, and now a slight chill crept into her voice. "I want to go to town. We can go together, I suppose. You can drop me off first." She didn't want to be alone with him? Was she going to consult Mr. Prentice? He pulled her chair out for her, and she said, "Thank you."

"What would you like to eat?" he asked, with more than usual solicitude.

"Just tea and toast," she said. He wanted to tell her she should eat more, but he couldn't suggest she needed to put more flesh on those lovely, small bones. She was perfect as she was.

He poured her tea, brought toast from the warming

rack, and put a pat of butter on her plate. He knew, without remembering when and where he had learned it, exactly how she liked her tea: strong and hot, with a little milk and two teaspoonfuls of sugar. He stood close to her, inhaled the scent of her clean hair, and made everything perfect for her. He was so wildly in love he could hardly breathe. Why had this affected him so deeply? It was her first time, not his.

He returned to his place but couldn't eat. He moved the book away, and she heard the slight rustle of the pages. "What is it?" she asked with casual interest.

"Still *The Last Temptation*," he said, and she nodded. He had told her about the new insight he had gained on the moneychangers in the temple, and she was waiting for the Braille edition from the State Library.

"That trash," her aunt said, scowling.

"It's literature," Mary Claire said. "Neil says it's a vivid picture of a very human Christ."

"Blasphemous trash. You shouldn't let him put ideas in your head. He's not a suitable influence."

"I'm sitting right here," he pointed out, but Mrs. St. James was unwilling to engage in any discussion with him directly.

They turned to plans for the day. He was included only because he was their driver. He wanted to drop Mrs. St. James where she wanted to go and stay with Mary Claire, but she said she was meeting a friend from church. He hadn't known she had any. He did remember a woman greeting her at the top of the steps the first day, but he had never noticed her chatting with any of the parishioners. She either came right out after the service or sat alone in the pew until he came for her.

If she did have a friend, would that be the person she would complain to of his betrayal, confide in about her feelings, ask for advice? She hadn't said yet where she wanted to be let off—it still might be Mr. Prentice's office.

Or the railroad station, suitcase in hand, to leave him forever?

"What was that?" Mrs. St. James asked, reacting to a slight sound. Mary Claire shrugged. Neil thought it had sounded like a door being slammed somewhere in the house.

He wanted to outlast Mrs. St. James so he could talk to Mary Claire, but the two women rose and left the room together to deal with the household accounts. He picked up his book and followed slowly, feeling as if he might be driven insane. It was not only that he was in suspense. He had braced himself for almost any reaction, but her complete silence was unnerving. She had so often been willing to tell him everything that came into her funny little head, and now she refused to talk about the one thing that mattered.

His ego was also beginning to bruise from the sense that last night had had no effect at all, had meant nothing to her. Was she made of ice, this little girl who had cried in his arms? It was as if it had been a dream—his or hers? Even a dream should have brought some reaction. She had said she sometimes had nightmares about the accident—was that why she had cried last night?

She and Mrs. St. James had disappeared into the study when he came out of the dining room, but the hall was not empty. Jane was waiting for him, her eyes blazing with fury. She slapped his face with every bit of

107

her considerable strength. Nothing was wrong with *her* aim. The blow definitely hurt him more than it hurt her. "You lousy bastard," she hissed.

He put a hand to his cheek. "What did she tell you?" he asked.

"She didn't have to tell me anything," she said angrily, keeping her voice low. "I'm not the blind one." In his concern for Mary Claire and his own guilt, he had forgotten that one of Jane's duties was to change the linen and make Mary Claire's bed. "You told me you weren't sleeping with her."

"I wasn't."

"Oh, well, that makes it all right, doesn't it? 'She's too young. She's not ready.' Bastard."

"I'm sorry. I should have told you, but—"

"But you're a goddamned cowardly shit," she said and turned on her heel.

Great. Now they were both angry with him.

He put ice on his face in hopes of forestalling a black eye he might have to explain. At least he didn't have to worry about Mary Claire seeing the bruise. He had time to wash the car before he was needed to drive them. The task was usually a relief to his feelings, but this time it didn't do anything for his state of mind—except to give him a sense that he was making her world as splendid as possible.

****

Mary Claire didn't tell Neil where she wanted to go until they were in Brierly. Her destination turned out to be the corner near the movie theater on Third Street. She was going to have lunch and see a matinee of *To Kill a Mockingbird* with her friend. He would have liked to discuss the book with her—he longed for that innocent conversation almost as much as he yearned to kiss her. "Don't get out," she said when he parked in front of the theater. She opened the door herself, but he got out anyway.

"Mary Claire," he said urgently, taking her hand to make sure she didn't trip on the curb, "we need to talk."

She stood still for a moment. "No," she said and turned away from him. A well-dressed woman in her thirties came forward to meet her.

While Mrs. St. James was spending an interminable time in a hat shop, Neil went into a tiny store that sold clocks and trinkets. Mary Claire's nineteenth birthday was coming up, and he had been searching for the perfect gift. A music box appealed to him as a likely choice, and on this afternoon with his mind in such turmoil, he happened on the perfect one. It was beautiful to the eye, but perhaps even more so to the sense of touch, with wood as smooth as silk, whorls of inlaid ivory, and soft velvet inside. It played Will Lamartine Thompson's "Softly and Tenderly," the hymn she had sung so sweetly at her grandfather's funeral.

When he returned to the theater to meet her, the trunk was full of parcels, and Mrs. St. James was complaining of the heat. Mary Claire was perfectly willing to talk—about *To Kill a Mockingbird*. She said it was wonderful, an excellent adaptation of the novel. She told him eagerly how important scenes had been handled, while her aunt sighed with boredom. Mary Claire didn't seem bothered at all by her inability to see the screen. Had her friend whispered necessary descriptions to her? He would have liked to be the one sitting beside her.

****

Mary Claire's silence on the one subject Neil wanted to discuss lasted for two more days. She skillfully evaded every opportunity for him to talk to her alone. Because they were together only at meals, they did talk about what they were reading or had read, until Mrs. St. James would snarl, "Will you two stop nattering about stupid books? You're ruining my appetite."

Neil also got the silent treatment from Jane, but at least he didn't have to sit with her at meals in the servants' hall—which had once been one of life's simple pleasures. She had left her mark, and he had no doubt Mrs. St. James had noticed his bruised face. She didn't deign to remark on it, but she regarded her niece with new respect. He didn't know whether Jane and Mary Claire were speaking to each other or not. If they weren't, he regretted damaging their once-promising friendship. If they were, it was uncomfortable to imagine what they might say to each other about him. He was in a deep hole of his own making.

Worse than the knowledge that he had lost Jane's affection was the recognition that it no longer mattered. It was Mary Claire he wanted. During the long nights, doubt and regret faded, and he longed to hold her again, to touch the soft fullness of her breasts, her smooth skin, and her silken hair, to taste her mouth and lose himself once more in her embracing warmth. Or if that were never to be, he would settle for a candid conversation, a chance to apologize and learn what she had felt and what she was feeling now.

On the third night, when he had begun to despair of any resolution, she came to his room. He woke when she opened the door. He said, "Mary Claire?" so she would know he was awake, and she tapped across the room to the bed. Because of the large window, his room had a little more light than hers, and he saw her put aside her cane and her robe before she came wordlessly into his arms.

Chapter Ten

Neil knew as soon as Mary Claire came into the dining room that this time a change *had* entered their relationship. They still hadn't talked much, but she had fallen asleep with her head on his chest, and this morning he detected a subtle, shy warmth in her manner that was definitely new. When he pulled her chair out, she murmured, "Thank you," in a soft voice that made him tingle. When he poured her tea, she touched his arm, and her hand lingered. She ate scrambled eggs and bacon and toast with more than her usual appetite. In front of Mrs. St. James, they talked about books and what was in the newspaper—the new pope and the nuclear test ban treaty—but when her aunt left in disgust at their pointless chatter, Mary Claire rose and came around the table to him.

She put a hand on his shoulder to orient herself and bent to give him a kiss. He was still a little tender from Jane's handiwork, but her lips sent a thrill through him. "Let's have a picnic," she said. She wore pink lipstick, and her hair was brushed back behind her perfect little ears. She was dressed in one of the more stylish outfits from the Whitman period and a pair of the shoes her aunt had selected.

"You look very pretty," he said. "I like your hair like that."

"You *did* notice," she said. "I stopped caring what I

looked like when I went blind, but now I care, because you can see me."

This sounded very promising.

****

As soon as Neil and Mary Claire were seated on the rocks in their special place, with the picnic basket on the ground beside them, she said, "We promised we would tell the truth here."

"And I told you I would always tell you the truth, here or anywhere."

"You didn't," she said bluntly. "You lied to me about Jane."

"No, I didn't. I didn't tell you everything—you asked for discretion—but I didn't lie."

She acknowledged his point with a brief nod.

"Is that why you've been so angry with me?" he asked.

"I wasn't angry," she said. "I had to think."

"Three days is a lot of thinking," he said. "Are you ready to talk about it now?"

"Yes."

His mind was so full of questions he didn't know where to start. He took her hand in both of his and kissed her cheek. He started with the most obvious and least important. "Did I hurt you?"

She started to shake her head, but she remembered where they were and said, "Yes, the first time, but not very much. It was all so strange and exciting that even the pain was special. I didn't know I would feel so much."

Relieved and touched, he kissed her again. "That's my brave girl," he said.

"I'm a woman now," she said proudly. "I wasn't

brave enough to marry The Boy, but—"

"Yes, you were. You just weren't stupid enough. Last night was very brave."

Mary Claire blushed like a young girl, but the smile was a woman's.

"You're much braver than I am," he said.

"You're afraid of bridges," she agreed. "You were a soldier, and you can see, and you're afraid of something that isn't even there."

"Maybe it's because I have no faith," he said.

"I have enough for both of us," she said, and then she sobered. "It's your turn to tell the truth," she said.

"Anything," he said. "I promise."

"When we were together—in bed—did you think about Jane?"

"No!" She jumped a little. "Lord, Mary Claire, how can you even ask that?"

She shrugged. "I know it was better with her. She's older. She knows things I don't."

"You'll learn," he said. He had never thought for a second of making comparisons. She lacked Jane's skill, of course—and her bad habits. She had so much to learn, and he would so enjoy teaching her—and no doubt he had much to learn from her too.

"She's beautiful," she said wistfully.

"How would you know?"

"I don't, but you do. She is, isn't she?"

"I don't want to talk about Jane. Envy is a sin. Do you remember asking me if I believed in fated true love?"

"And blah-blah-blah."

"I said I believed in love that grows between people who are right for each other. We're all wrong for each other. You know that, don't you? I am way too old for you."

"I don't care," she said. "We both love books, and we can agree to disagree about religion."

"We're still wrong for each other," he said.

"Then it must be blah-blah-blah."

He laughed. "What I'm trying to say, sweetheart—and no, I'm not being condescending this time—is that even if it is blah-blah-blah, you aren't stuck with me. I'm sorry I broke the agreement—"

"*We* broke the agreement," she said. "I could have stopped you. I could have said no."

"Thank you for saying so. In any case, we can't get an annulment. It will have to be a divorce, but it's still yours for the asking. You should go back to school and meet young men you'll have more in common with."

"Because you don't want to be married to me? Because I'm blind and too young and skinny?"

"Because I don't want you to be bound to an old duffer like me. Your blindness doesn't matter. What matters is your sweet, brave, funny little heart. I wouldn't mind fattening you up a little, but you're gorgeous exactly the way you are."

"No lies, Neil."

"I'm not lying. I'm so in love with you right now that I might be delusional, but I'm not lying."

"You're in love with me?"

"Apparently. Which is all the more reason why I need you to think straight. Don't make a decision out of obligation or jealousy or to keep your inheritance."

"So is this the honeymoon period?"

He had to laugh. "I suppose it is."

"When it's over, will you leave me alone?"

"I'm not your Uncle Marcus. The question is: do you want me to leave you alone? The agreement still stands—I have no conjugal rights. Everything is up to you. You didn't sign away any of your rights. You have rights, but no obligations."

She thought about it. "So if there was something I didn't like, you wouldn't do it anymore?"

"Was there?"

She didn't answer, but her cheeks flushed pink.

"Oh, Lord, Sunny—no, of course not. You should have said something. I'm sorry. You can tell me what you like and what you don't…Or show me. Anything else?"

"You really wouldn't?"

"Not if you don't like it."

"And then you would go and do it with Jane instead?"

"Mary Claire! Is that what you think of me? For starters, she may never speak to me again. Even if she forgives me, what we had is over and done with. I know it's hard for you to understand that what matters so much between us could be so unimportant between Jane and me, but it was." He knew unimportant was the wrong word, but he would feel guilty about Jane in any case.

"So you wouldn't mind if I gave her notice?"

"I most certainly would. None of this is her fault. She's been a friend to both of us. She's an amoral creature, but she's honest. What I did was bad enough—don't make it worse by being unkind to her. Let her look after your aunt, if you'd prefer, but don't fire her. She may not want it right now, but she needs this job. She has a sick mother to support, and even if you give her a good reference—"

Mary Claire, being Mary Claire, said, "Her mother is sick? Does she live in Brierly? Can we help her? Can we send her something, or—does she have a good doctor? We could have Dr. Young—"

"I think she has everything she needs. Just don't fire Jane. Even in romantic fantasies—and blah-blah-blah—people get hurt. Let's try not to hurt her any more than we have."

"You really don't want to…do anything with her?"

"No. Now that you and I are really married, now that we are truly husband and wife—assuming you are willing for that to continue—there can't be anyone else. Only you."

"What if I'm not enough?"

"Oh, my precious girl, of course you are *enough*. You are the world."

"Am I?" She made a quick, eager move toward him, her lips parted in amazement.

"Yes. You are the world." He turned her face gently to him and took off her sunglasses. He moved so the sun wouldn't fall on her face and gazed into her sightless eyes and kissed the scars that had helped make her who she was. "I love you, Mary Claire St. James DeWinter Vincent. Will you marry me? In church, in front of your God and the entire world?"

"He's your God too."

"No, no lies, remember?"

She nodded. "Yes, I will marry you, in the presence of God and everyone, even if you are an atheist and thirty-eight years old and afraid of bridges and horses, but—"

"I did tell you I love you, didn't I?"

"Yes, you did. It just so happens I love you too. But we can't have a Nuptial Mass unless you want to convert."

"You know I can't. Don't marry me thinking that will change."

"If we tell Father Halloran you're a Christian, he'll marry us without the Mass. You don't have to tell him the rest. Where are my glasses? I feel naked without them." He handed them to her and retrieved the package he had tucked into the picnic basket.

"I have a present for you," he said. "It was supposed to be for your birthday, but I couldn't wait. It can double as an engagement gift."

"I love presents," she said. She took it eagerly and managed to figure out the way past the ribbon and tape. He sat back and resisted the urge to help. When she had the little box in her hands she explored it thoughtfully. "Oh, Neil," she said. "It's lovely. It feels so nice, so special."

"It's ivory inside the depressions," he said. "Open it."

She opened it, and the hymn began to play. She touched the velvet. "It's perfect," she said. She put out her hand to find his cheek, and their lips touched in a long, sweet kiss.

"Happy birthday," he said. "It's only a little early."

"When I'm nineteen I'll be half your age," she said. "I'm gaining on you, but I'll never catch up. When I'm forty, you'll be sixty."

"I'll die twenty years before you will," he said, "and you'll have to marry The Boy next time." He meant it as a joke, but she looked stricken.

"You would do that?" she asked. "You would leave

me?"

"Oh, Sunny," he said. "You'll break my heart."

"I have a gift for you, too," she said. She took a folded paper out of her pocket. "This is the right one, isn't it?" She unfolded it and showed him the wordy legal document Mr. Prentice had drawn up for them.

"The agreement?"

"Yes," she said, and methodically tore it into pieces.

"That will give me rights to your money and—"

"I know what it gives you rights to," she said.

****

While they were eating sandwiches and fruit, Mary Claire said, "We should get married as soon as possible."

"Why?" Neil asked. "Your aunt has already been cheated out of one lavish wedding, and these things take time."

"She won't like the location or the groom, so she has nothing to say about it. I do want Phillip to come, and my father if he's up to it, but otherwise sooner is better."

"You don't want a fancy white dress and engraved invitations and all that? It's my intention that this will be your last wedding—at least in my lifetime."

"I don't think I can wear white now," she said. "Anyway, I would like to be married in the Church as soon as possible, because—oh, I should have asked, before I said yes, if this would be a problem for you."

"What?"

"I won't do anything to keep from having a baby. Maybe the rhythm method. It's what you get when you marry a good Catholic girl.

"I'm a little old to be starting a family."

"I'm sorry," she said. "We can compromise on a lot of things, but birth control isn't one of them."

"When did you get so tough?" he asked. "I guess I'll have to take my chances. It may not happen any time soon—or at all." Maybe he could change her mind.

"That's not what they told us in Catholic school," she said, smiling.

"What did they tell you about sex in Catholic school?"

"My 'wifely duty'? They were wrong."

"You shameless hussy," he said.

She laughed. "If I do have a baby…"

"Are you trying to scare me?"

She patted his hand like a mother comforting a child. "What's your father's name?" she asked.

"Frederick."

"Oh, no, that won't do, will it? Would you object to Michael?"

Epilogue

September 1964

Mary Claire had moved into Neil's room, the one with the window seat and the now-crowded bookshelves, so her old room, with its sturdy four-poster bed and blue-patterned wallpaper, was available as a makeshift maternity suite. She was having the baby at home because the hospital rules would have kept Neil outside.

"One more big push, Mrs. V," said Dr. Young, and the baby slid out, slippery and red, into his big, capable hands. "A perfect little boy," he said and laid him on his mother's chest.

"Neil!" she cried. "Look at him. Tell me." She touched the baby's face gently, wonderingly.

"He has a lot of very dark hair," he told her. "He looks like you. He has your dimple."

She found the dimple and moved on. "No, look," she said. "His nose is like yours, but very small."

He bent to kiss her and then touched a finger to his son's soft, tiny hand. Michael Austin Vincent squirmed and closed his unfocused blue eyes. He yawned.

"He's big, isn't he?" Mary Claire asked. "Does he have all his fingers and toes?" She cradled one small foot in her hand.

"Every one," he said. "They're perfect, so tiny and

so perfect. He has fingernails too. I love you."

"I love you too. Aren't we lucky?"

"We are," he said. He leaned forward for a closer view of the baby. Michael opened his eyes and blinked at the light. Although he surely couldn't see clearly yet, he appeared to be staring right into his father's eyes.

In that moment Neil knew he had crossed the one bridge he needed to cross—the one built with the love of Mary Claire DeWinter—and this must be what it would be like to feel the presence of God.

A word about the author...

Linda Griffin retired as Fiction Librarian for the San Diego Public Library to spend more time on her writing, and her work has been published in numerous journals. In addition to the three Rs—reading, writing, and research—she enjoys Scrabble, movies, and travel. *Bridges* is her fifth Wild Rose Press novel.

http://www.lindagriffinauthor.com/